The moment was awkward....

She removed her boots and socks and then her petticoat, shivering in her woolen-stockinged feet.

"Stay near the fire till you're warm." A muscle flicked along Brant's cheek. Rain drizzled down his temples.

"What about you? You're wet too."

He swung around, bold and sure of himself. His gaze trailed down her face and settled on her blouse. He growled then, like the grizzly he appeared to be. Then, in one daring move, he reached up and pulled her down to his lap. She gasped at his speed.

Their lips touched softly. With another yank he kissed her hard, swooped her off her feet and onto the soft rug by the fire.

Laid out on her back beneath his body, she felt her pulse come alive with a powerful beat. Her stomach quaked. How could she want a man this much? Someone she couldn't get involved with? Someone who'd been dead wrong for her siste~~~~~~ her too?

But when he kisse~~~~~~ feel like hurt.

ALASKAN RENEGADE

Kate Bridges

First published in Great Britain 2012
by Mills & Boon, an imprint of Harlequin (UK) Limited.
Harlequin (UK) Limited, Eton House, 18-24 Paradise Road,
Richmond, Surrey TW9 1SR

© Katherine Haupt 2009

ISBN: 978 0 263 89221 5

Harlequin (UK) policy is to use papers that are natural, renewable and recyclable products and made from wood grown in sustainable forests. The logging and manufacturing process conform to the legal environmental regulations of the country of origin.

Printed and bound in Spain
by Blackprint CPI, Barcelona

Award-winning and multi-published author **Kate Bridges** was raised in rural Canada, and her stories reflect her love for wide-open spaces, country sunshine and the Rocky Mountains. She loves writing adventurous tales about the men and women who tamed the West. Prior to becoming a full-time writer, Kate worked as a paediatric intensive care nurse. She often includes compelling medical situations in her novels. Later in her education she studied architecture, and worked as a researcher on a television design programme. She recently completed postgraduate studies in comedy screenwriting, and in her spare time writes screenplays. Kate's novels have been translated into nine languages, studied in over a dozen colleges on their commercial fiction courses, and are sold worldwide. She lives in the beautiful cosmopolitan city of Toronto with her family. To find out more about Kate's books, and to sign up for her free online newsletter, please visit www.katebridges.com

Novels by the same author:

THE DOCTOR'S HOMECOMING
THE SURGEON
THE ENGAGEMENT
THE PROPOSITION
THE CHRISTMAS GIFTS
(part of *A Season of the Heart*)
THE BACHELOR
THE COMMANDER
KLONDIKE DOCTOR
SHOTGUN VOWS
(part of *Western Weddings*)
KLONDIKE WEDDING
KLONDIKE FEVER
WANTED IN ALASKA

This book is dedicated to the Toronto Romance Writers
with much appreciation
for the many years of friendship and support.

Chapter One

Skagway, District of Alaska, late August 1899

That familiar and arrogant way he moved captured her attention. Wearing a tan leather vest and black shirt that barely spanned his wide shoulders, Brant MacQuaid strode down the path as though he still thought he could part the Red Sea. His granite eyes flickered at the stagecoach driver, then he turned and headed straight for her. Her heart leaped. He'd changed a great deal in the five years since Victoria Windhaven had last laid eyes on him.

He was more of a man.

I don't care, she told herself. He was one of three men who'd deserted her at a time when she'd needed him to stay. She wouldn't give him the satisfaction of knowing how devastated she'd been.

With her pulse rushing, Victoria shuffled beneath her skirts and stood in the morning light that slanted over the livery stables and cast shadows on their well-oiled stagecoach. Stable hands around them calmly pitched straw and walked horses, unaware of her moment of reckoning.

Her partner on this journey, young medical student Cooper Sullivan, was huffing in exertion as he tried to swing his suitcases up beside the driver.

Brant reached her side, still a head taller but so much more filled out. Last she'd heard, he was hundreds of miles away, hired as a trail guide in the Klondike. Maybe he'd even tried his own hand at staking gold.

She sucked in the dusty air. Fighting for poise, she gripped her medical bags. "What are you doing here?"

"Morning." His voice was as deep and razor-sharp as she remembered. He tilted his hat in mock salute. "Pleasure to see you, too, Victoria." His eyes cornered hers.

"Rumor was you were in Dawson."

"Old rumor."

He was as annoying as ever. What did it matter? She was leaving town and owed him nothing. Not even the slightest social grace.

He looked over her shoulder toward the inside of Colburne Stables. Wasn't even able to meet her eyes. Maybe his guilt had finally caught up to him. The cad.

His gaze returned to her face.

She tilted one shoulder at him. "This stage is private. If you've bought a ticket, keep it for the next one."

"Don't need a ticket." Then he added in a more personal tone, "You're a long way from St. Louis."

She ignored his attempt to get reacquainted. "Let me say this again. This coach is for the medical team heading to Glitter Mountain."

"I heard you became a nurse."

"And I never heard what more became of you." Not until last year, but she'd rather play innocent than admit she'd exchanged a thread of gossip about him.

"If I thought you cared about my well-being, I'd tell you."

Now he really was too much.

With a whirl of her skirts, she set down one of her bags and opened the coach door. She called over her shoulder in a dismissive manner, "I'll be leaving town for two or three weeks, so you won't have to worry about that. Enjoy your solitude."

"Can't say I will."

She wheeled back to him again. Hot sunshine

blasted her cheeks beneath her cowboy hat. The hat was much sturdier and offered more protection from the weather than a bonnet. "What do you mean?"

"I'm going with you."

She squared her jaw. "I've just explained. This coach is for me, that young man, and—" she peered around Brant's obnoxiously wide frame, looking for another man "—our bodyguard."

Something in his dark eyes intensified, and her stomach fluttered in a silent warning. "Oh, no." Alarmed, she stepped back a few paces. "Don't tell me. Please don't tell me…"

"Got hired last night."

"What happened to Harry? He went with me in the spring." She peered desperately around the stables. "He knows the backwoods up and down."

"Expecting his brother on a ship, any day now. Harry prefers to stay here and greet him."

"What about John?" Her voice rose another octave. "John Abraham?"

"He's already up there. Took a group on an expedition to the mountains, looking for gold. My orders are to bring you there. He'll bring you back."

"But the deputy marshal…" Her mouth ran dry.

"Go ahead and talk to him. He's the one who hired me."

Her stomach tightened into a lump. He peered over her shoulder again. What was he looking at?

Were the men behind her more interesting than what she had to say? She was speaking about his job.

His focus returned. Those sharp gray eyes she'd once found charming were now untrustworthy. "Up to you. You could make your patients on the trail wait a day or two, till they find you another body-guard. Or you can relax—for once in your life—and accept my services."

The nerve.

Outrage pounded through her, just as Cooper stepped up beside them.

He was a slender young man in a tweed wool vest, studying to be a doctor and here for the summer from Philadelphia.

He craned his head at Brant. "You qualified, mister?"

Brant smirked.

"Land's sake," she sputtered, her thoughts still on Brant's insulting comment. "You're the one who was wound up so tight—"

Before she could finish, he pulled a gun from his holster so fast at her, she squealed and dropped her remaining bag. He leaped toward her. She shut her eyes for a second, but heard no gunshot. Just the sound of his footsteps raced behind her.

She opened her lids and wheeled around at the commotion. Men inside the livery stable halted in the midst of their chores to watch Brant jump over the stall boards and leap at three men.

"Stop!" Brant hollered.

But two of the men ran. The one holding the reins of a horse swung at Brant. Brant ducked, then jumped up and punched the stranger in the jaw.

She yelped.

Always looking for a fight. Always.

When the man hit the floor, two stable hands rushed to keep him down as Brant pursued the others. He caught them as they raced through the back doors into the corral. He collared one, wheeled him around and slugged him in the gut. When the second stranger doubled over, Brant raced to catch the third, twenty feet into the field.

Brant shouted again, "Stop! Horse thief!"

The man kept running. Brant reached him, yanked him by the shoulder and punched him, too.

She closed her eyes at the fighting. When she opened them again, the stable hands had taken over the scene, patting Brant on the back, getting the story from him.

She heard only snatches. "…recognized one from Dawson…wanted for bank robbery."

Victoria sank onto the floor of the stagecoach behind her, grappling for air. Her heartbeat roared through her chest. Cooper stood with his hands on his hips, equally thunderstruck.

How was she going to deal with this man? A barbarian, the way he used his fists and his body.

Blazes, why did he have to be so good at violence?

She did a quick calculation of time. She was already starting a week late due to the delays here in Skagway—the banker's broken ankle, heart trouble for the minister's wife and the fatal stroke of the poor tinsmith. Yesterday, trappers had told her there was already snow in the mountains. It would reach the valleys soon. There was no more time to delay this journey. Folks depended on her, since a nurse only made it up the coast twice a year. And this trip was different.

The most vital reason for going to Glitter Mountain was to check on the gold miners injured in the cave-in.

It had already taken a couple of weeks for the news to reach them in Skagway. She had to see how the broken bones were mending, and ensure the men were getting out of bed every day, moving their muscles and working their lungs.

A bodyguard was essential. The trail was thick with dangerous strangers—failed gold miners looking to rob anyone they crossed, men who hadn't laid their eyes on a woman for two years, and criminals who'd fled justice from the lower states.

She studied the group of men before her. With

softer words, the stable hands indicated they'd haul the three thieves to the jailhouse by themselves if Brant was in a hurry to leave with her.

Brant dusted off his black Stetson and returned to the coach. His black hair, vivid in the sun, dipped around his ears. And there was that long, irritating stride. When he faced her again, she noted the tiny new-to-her creases at his eyes, the leaner jaw and the calm control he had over the situation. He hadn't been so calm in St. Louis.

Damn him for his competence.

He gazed at her, then Cooper. "You satisfied with the deputy marshal's pick? Or you want to call for someone else?"

She jumped to her feet, her starched blouse still crisp from the morning iron.

The excitement and fear of what she'd just witnessed raced through her muscles. The moment throbbed with unspoken words. But she didn't want to give him an inch.

Cooper broke the stalemate. "I guess you are qualified, mister."

She pushed past this…this hired gun to get her bags. "Of course he is. Used to be a bounty hunter. With the same killer instinct as a rattlesnake."

She didn't mean the words as a compliment. But with a vexing nod of amusement, the familiar gunman tugged his hat onto his head and had the gall to dismiss her to speak to the driver. She grated at the sound of her name coming from his throat.

"Thank you kindly, Victoria."

"What took you so long?" Victoria snapped at Brant from inside the stagecoach as he approached forty-five minutes later.

Hell, he thought, adjusting his hat as he eased into the tight quarters, this woman needed to relax. If she were a porcupine, her quills would be in a spiked position, ready to strike.

He shifted his long legs opposite hers. The driver, Gus Newly, a thick man with scruffy gray hair, shut the door.

Brant tossed his hat on the seat beside him and leaned forward, nice and close. He jammed one knee firmly between hers. "The deputy marshal wanted a written statement. He also needed to speak to the three other witnesses." He leaned back in frustration. His boots shuffled on the planks. "And I did not appreciate you trouncing in and asking about John Abraham when we were in the middle of the statements."

"I wanted to make sure he's meeting us at Glitter Mountain and taking us home. You don't expect me to just take your word for it." She drew in her rib cage, yanked on the fabrics of her skirt and tucked her knees away from his, avoiding all contact.

On the other side of her, the boy-doctor hastily looked away from Brant's glare and amused himself by staring out the scratched glass window, all the while stealing glances at Victoria.

Brant tried not to watch the medical student watching her, but there was little else to amuse him.

What a strange couple, thought Brant. They looked too young to be medical saviors. Not the choicest companions Brant had ever had. Certainly not the most pleasing to the spirit.

The stage rolled forward and they were off.

She might've approved of him years ago when he'd first come into her life, but she certainly didn't approve of him now. He sucked on that for a while, as sour as it was. All the more incentive to keep his real reason for heading to Glitter Mountain to himself.

In St. Louis, he'd done what he had to under the circumstance, even if she hadn't liked it. Faced with the same choices, he'd do it again.

Straining to hold his tongue, he nudged his hat forward, swung his boots at an angle over the threadbare cushion beside him and tried to get some shut-eye.

He ignored her loud scowl and slept with his hand near one of his Colt revolvers. He enjoyed the weight of his holster as it dipped around his hips.

Next thing he knew, he awoke with a jostle.

"First stop," said the doctor with the fuzz that substituted for a mustache.

Brant swung his legs out of the way. "Sure thing, doc."

"Oh, no, no, no." Cooper adjusted his string tie and yanked on his bowler hat. "I'm not a doctor till I get my license. And I'm three years away from that." He blushed.

Honest to God, Brant had never seen a man blush before. It came in blotches beside his ears.

The young man grabbed his medical bag and leaped out.

Victoria fiddled with her bags on the luggage rack above their seats. Brant jumped up to help her.

He fumbled for something neutral to say, perhaps even pleasant. "There still a shortage of doctors in Skagway?"

"Yeah. There's just me and two other nurses. Plus the three medical students for the summer."

"I reckon you feel lucky, then…being under that young man's guidance."

Victoria angled past his body, close enough for him to smell the soap she'd used for her glossy brown hair.

Her green eyes flashed. "I'm afraid the only thing Mr. Sullivan has mastered so far in his studies is a chart of the human body. He can name more muscles than I knew existed. Oh, and he also knows

the hierarchy on the board of directors at his Philadelphia hospital." She looked Brant up and down
and shook her head. "I would feel a lot luckier if he
had some experience behind him. Or a willingness
to want some. Because what he avoids at every turn
is dealing with a wound deeper than a scratch."

With that insane pronouncement, she slid by
Brant, her warm elbow grazing his chest, and
hopped off the stage.

At their first stop, Victoria tried to coax the
medical student as they stood outside the cluster
of cabins. Trees whooshed in the wind around them.
Gus and Brant were tending to the horses. "Mrs.
Tobin seems to have a problem with her bladder.
Think how much you'd learn."

"Please, could you do the exam? It's not my…
She'll feel more comfortable with a woman."

"The more you do, the more comfortable you'll
feel."

"There's another patient here who needs his ears
checked. The ears are mine. You handle the lady,
and later, tell me what you see."

Victoria sighed, turned around and trudged back
into the cabin. Although she'd made the trip without
him in May, she was hoping he'd see this journey
as a wonderful opportunity for learning.

He'd be headed back to Philadelphia in three

weeks, back to the books he was so good at memorizing. And the father who had made the decision for Cooper to become a doctor. Victoria wondered if Cooper himself had decided that was what he wanted to be.

She took a couple of deep breaths and went back into the cabin to examine her patient.

Half an hour later, Victoria exited, thankful it was only a mild bladder condition that could be alleviated with herbs and tea. She'd enjoyed visiting with Mrs. Tobin and wished there were more women in Skagway she could befriend.

A new lump of gold weighted down her pocket. Some folks were so generous. She held up the loaf of bread she was kindly given, wrapped in a linen napkin. "Thank you for the fresh bread! Smells heavenly!"

"My pleasure, Victoria!" Mrs. Tobin, thirty years old with two youngsters clinging to her apron, waved from the door.

"Well?" Victoria asked Cooper as she strode to the coach. "What was wrong with the ear? Too much wax?"

"Yes, ma'am. As you predicted. I...I had his brother flush it out." He turned and dashed for the coach, yards ahead of her.

His brother? Victoria shoved her tongue into the side of her cheek, praying for patience. How would Cooper learn any clinical skills if he didn't attempt them?

"Come," he shouted from the open door of the conveyance. "Tell me what you observed with your patient."

She made her way toward him as Brant's shadow crossed her path. His broad silhouette cast a powerful presence. "All done?"

She brought two fingers to her chin, rubbed and nodded.

"You might go easy on him," said Brant.

Had he been eavesdropping on her and Cooper?

"How would you know what I'm thinking about him?"

"It's written on your face. The way the top of your nose wrinkles between your eyebrows. At one time, you used to look at me like that."

Annoyed that he was mentioning the past, she gaped up at him.

"Yeah, just like that." Brant planted a hand along his holster. "He might be scared, but he came, didn't he?"

Cooper was trying. At the start of the summer, he hadn't even known the difference between the types of suturing patterns. She'd shown him the running stitch, the figure eight and the interrupted stitch.

That, however, was none of Brant's business.

She slid her hand into the back of her collar and massaged her tense neck. "This'll be a long journey. Please don't tell me you're going to take his side in everything."

His eyes twinkled with amusement. "I'll weigh things, argument by argument."

It was a weak attempt at humor.

"And besides," he said, his lips barely concealing laughter, "he's sweet on you."

"What?"

"Don't tell me you don't notice the way he looks at you. Shimmies up to your side in the coach. Pants at every word you say."

Her jaw dropped. What? Cooper? She peered past Brant's shoulder to the young man staring at her from the opened coach door. Oh, heavens, the sharp look in his eye…

She shrank in her boots and slid back behind Brant's large shoulders, hiding from the medical student.

How long had this been going on? He was years younger! Well, not that many years…perhaps only one, if that. One in chronological years, but ten in maturity.

Just as she was trying to get her bearing on this bit about Cooper, Brant raised the subject she was hoping he'd never bring up again.

The smile on his lips faded. His tone was rich and deep. "How's your sister?"

Victoria gulped, assaulted by the memory of that awful month after Brant had deserted them all in St. Louis. She snapped past him toward the coach, her medical bag jerking with her movements, determined not to let him get to her. "Seeing how you left her at the altar, that's none of your business!"

Chapter Two

Five years was a long time for Victoria to hold a grudge.

Several hours later when they stopped at a road-house for the evening, Brant was still resenting her comments.

What did she expect from him now? That he'd roll over and kiss her boots? Write a letter to her sister, Sarah, and explain? Explain what? He'd said it all before he'd left, and it was the Windhaven family who'd chosen not to accept his apologies, nor his explanations.

Not to mention his own family. He never regretted telling his father, the governor of Missouri, how he'd felt about refusing to follow in anyone's political footsteps, but his ma… Her disappointment still ached in the sore part of his heart.

Trying to shake it off, Brant walked one of the horses to a far tree and hitched it. Now that the sun was wavering at the horizon, a chill clung to the air. The temperature had dropped ten degrees and they'd each put on their leather coats.

Cooper edged forward with his suitcase. It was as shiny and polished as his new medical bag, Brant noted. Cooper had the means to buy a nice one, but it had rarely been opened.

"You sure you won't sleep inside?" Cooper scratched his youthful cheek.

"They're short on rooms."

"Oh." Cooper looked to the log house surrounded by aspens and scraggly cedars. "We could share—"

"No, thanks."

Rebutted, Cooper clutched his bag. He turned around as Victoria made her way over, clad in a long leather duster that had a feminine cut to it, sashaying and pointing to the rack above the coach as if Brant was her private footman.

"I'd like that trunk inside with me."

Firm. Polite. Condescending.

Brant bristled at her manner. "It'll be fine out here."

"Someone could take it while you're sleeping."

He shrugged.

She must not have liked his reaction, for she tongued the inside of her cheek, and raised those pretty eyebrows for effect. "It's full of medical supplies. I want it near my bedside."

He saluted her lightly. "Yes, ma'am."

Cooper snickered beneath his feathery mustache. Victoria clicked her tongue at the young man.

"I'm not laughin' at you," Cooper hurried to tell her, "I'm laughin' at him."

Brant reared back. "Me?"

"You're always out of sorts with her." Cooper headed back to the inn. "Good night."

Victoria eyed Brant beneath the brim of her cowboy hat. Her voice had a military drill to it. "Will you carry it in for me, or must I bother Gus?"

Their driver was busy building a campfire in a clearing by the forest where he and Brant would sleep for the night.

"I got it," Brant said, "I got it."

She twirled on the heel of her boot, her wavy brown hair lifting at the ends, and made for the door. "Room 108."

Gus looked over and lifted his shoulder in a gesture of sympathy.

After Brant settled his bedroll next to the fire, preparing his own things first and stretching out the time as long as he could, he finally heaved the heavy treasure chest to his shoulders and took the few steps to the front door. He strode past the front desk and down the hallway.

The door to Room 108 was slightly ajar.

Victoria was humming inside but stopped when he kicked open the door. "Coming through."

"Right here." She pointed to the gap on the floor between her narrow bed and the wall. She was no longer wearing her duster or hat, and part of her blouse had pulled out of her skirt. The cotton fabric hung loosely around her right hip.

She made an interesting picture, rumpled femininity in an otherwise stiff and proper demeanor.

The place she pointed at was not exactly the easiest one to maneuver. He squeezed past her and eased the trunk along his thigh, over his knee and down his boot to the floor planks.

"I expect you back in the morning, six o'clock sharp, to load it up again."

"Please, Brant," he corrected her.

He heard her sharp intake of breath as he adjusted the trunk against the wall. Straightening up, he added, "I didn't hear a please. Your mother didn't raise you to be rude."

"You have an awful lot of nerve, bringing up my family." She took a huge step away from him and waved him to the door. "Please…leave."

He glared at her. "So you do know how to use that word." With a huff, he made for the door, then stopped and swung around. "What is it with you?"

She puckered her mouth and turned back to unpacking her suitcase on the bed.

"I couldn't go through with the wedding, okay?" he said. "I apologized to your sister. Apologized to your father. Your mother. What more do you want?"

"Nothing," she snapped, and flung a folded blouse to her bed. "I want nothing from you."

"You got it." He muttered beneath his breath and stepped over the threshold. Surprising him, she stomped over and slammed the door against his shoulder. In a heated response, he pushed hard against the pine slab. She yelped and slammed hard against it, and he lunged to push it back, the two of them jarring the door back and forth between them an inch at a time, both desperate to win the battle of who controlled the door.

He struggled to gain hold of his footing, but the pine slab pressed hard against his shoulder and wouldn't budge. Damn, she was strong when she was mad.

He groaned. "What on earth did I do to deserve your wrath?"

"You didn't apologize to me!"

Her comment surprised the hell out of him. He stopped pushing.

She must have stopped struggling on the other side of the door, too, for the door released and hit the back wall with a loud bang. He turned around and faced her through the opening.

Her breathing came quick and shallow. Her long hair sat tussled over one breast, and her blouse was now fully yanked out of her skirts.

She'd only been a girl of thirteen when he'd first started courting her sister. Sixteen when he came back to say goodbye. Giggling and whispering most of the time he'd known her. Hell, she was even hoping for an engagement herself, he recalled, to a young preacher who'd just started his ministry.

Her marriage hadn't materialized, either. That much was obvious. But he wondered why.

He found it hot standing here, the two of them in some sort of face-off.

Watching her eyes sparkle up at him in an angry glimmer made him think of home. Family and people he once knew a lifetime ago. He'd written home twice in the past two years, both times at Christmas, but hadn't gotten a response. In all fairness, he was never in one place for long so it would've been difficult to get a reply. But he'd been all over Alaska and the Yukon for over a year, and no one had contacted him here. They could've left a message in Skagway.

His parents didn't approve of his choice of work and had disowned him.

But this woman... She was soft and warm and

familiar, all the things he hadn't realized how much he'd craved till he'd laid eyes on her this morning.

He'd hurt her, and he didn't even know how. She was a kid back then, not old enough to fill out a corset.

She sure as hell filled one out now.

A muscle in her cheek flickered. He stepped closer, a fingertip away, and reached down and grazed the soft skin of her jaw. She turned her cheek away, refusing his touch, but that only made him hungrier. He cupped her cheek and ear and tugged her back toward him.

"I'm sorry," he whispered.

"It's too late." She pulled her head away again. Then more gruffly, "I don't accept your apology."

It was the fire in her voice that tripped him. The push of raw emotions, the glistening of pretty eyes that denounced him and all he used to be, that made him burn with an urge to challenge her.

He swooped down and kissed her on the mouth. The wench grew still. He moved his lips over the sweet pleasure, working his fingers through her hair and clamping his large hand over the nape of her downy neck. Skin so smooth and pure, he had no right to touch it.

He felt her stir, her lips move against his. She murmured softly and her hand came up between them. It was a touch that surprised him, one he'd never expected from this woman. He'd never thought of her beyond being Sarah's younger sister, the one who was never serious about her studies, who never stopped long enough to listen to old folks complaining about their health. It hadn't seemed likely she would become a nurse.

Her gentle hand slid up his chest and he expected her to stroke his face. Instead, she slapped him cold.

He stumbled back. His cheek stung. "Why'd you do that?"

"Did that kiss remind you of Sarah?"

"You've got a rung missing on your ladder, woman."

"How dare you try to seduce me!"

"If I was trying, I'd be successful."

She pointed to the door. "Get out!"

"I thought you'd never ask."

He stomped out, and the door slammed behind him with a loud bang on his heel, followed by the sound of her boot kicking the wood. She was insane.

How could anyone hold this much animosity?

Heaving with turmoil himself, he strode down the hall and out the door, hurled down the steps, and aimed for the ring of cottonwoods beyond the camp.

Dammit!

He slammed his hat against the trunk of a passing tree. Put him in his place, would she? He'd see about that. Seduce her? Ha! He didn't even find her attractive!

As soon as she opened her mouth, every word grated on his nerves.

He tried to calm down as he settled around the fire, talking to Gus about trivial matters.

Two hours later, though, Brant's head was still throbbing when he thought of her. He kicked his boots over his bedroll and pressed his shoulder against the hard ground, longing for sleep. He'd stay as far away as possible from that spitting cobra.

"Did you know Brant spent six months panning for gold last summer?" Squinting in the sunshine early the next morning, Cooper nudged Victoria's arm.

"Mmm?" She pretended not to be the least bit interested in either man as she jostled in the stage-coach, this time careful not to sit directly across from Brant. She had tricked Cooper into sitting across from the hired gun. Let the two men knock knees together, not her. Yet, knowing Cooper might have feelings for her made her anxious not to sit too close to him, either. And she tried not to let Brant know that she was feeling uneasy about Cooper.

Oh, heavens. She exhaled and tried to loosen up. It was just past breakfast and they'd already made one stop. No one had needed medical attention in the two cabins that were filled with the wonderful aroma of baked onions and fried fish.

"Six months," Cooper repeated. "He was panning for gold."

Brant looked over from the window, then back out again, ignoring Cooper's comment.

"Is that so? I'm glad Gus is driving," she said, trying to change the subject. "He's such a good driver."

Who gave a damn about Brant? She tried not to remember the way his lips had felt on hers last night. She glared out the cracks of the window to the wooded edge of the trail. It was like a cage, this contraption, a rough wagon with a lid on it, certainly nothing as civilized as the silky coaches her father owned. Granted, it was newly built from Alaskan wood, but rudimentary. Supplies in Alaska were so scarce, nearly everything except wood was imported and reused a hundred times over. Including the cracked glass and the iron wheels.

Cooper persisted. "Tell her, Brant. Tell her how you witnessed nuggets the size of snowballs being hauled out of the rivers."

"Snowballs can be very small," she said, then bit her lip to stop herself from saying anything more. Any reply on her part would indicate interest, and she was not interested.

Brant thumbed the buttons of his shirt. "You used to roll them quite big, as I recall."

Say nothing, she warned herself. She leaned forward and unbuckled her medical bag, pretending to be interested in the gauze bandages.

"You two know each other?" Cooper's voice rippled with awe. He pressed his face closer, freckles splattered over his cheeks, his nose creased with enthusiasm.

"Hmm," she muttered, when the other party didn't reply.

"Then you must know how he got so good with his gun!"

She rummaged deeper into her stock and rolled her eyes at the young man's adulation.

She wasn't biting. She removed the precious, year-old *British Medical Journal* that Cooper had given her at the start of the summer, sat back on the flattened cushion and leafed through its dog-eared pages.

"Oh, a new tonic for diarrhea," she said, reading from the journal and pretending to be deeply interested, but hoping to shut down the conversation.

Cooper brushed her skirt as he peered over her arm. "Yes, that one works quite well, I'm told. I'll ship you a crate when I return to Philadelphia."

She brightened with pleasure. The lad was a good source of needed medical supplies, if nothing else. Was she using him, in a sense, every time she took him up on his offers? She didn't think so. These supplies weren't for her; they would be used to nurse others. How could that be selfish?

"Or you could visit Philadelphia sometime," Cooper murmured. "And come get it yourself."

Victoria felt the heat rise up her chest. He was so young, and she didn't feel the least bit attracted to him. He'd make a charming beau for some other young lady, but Cooper's interest in her was wasted.

She looked out the window, past the scratches of the thick glass, and ignored the young's man suggestion.

Brant coughed, though, and she could very well imagine the irritating little smirk on his face. He shifted those long hard legs that seemed to always be in the way, and even though he wasn't sitting directly across from her, still managed to plant one knee a quarter-inch away from hers.

"Lovely idea," Brant said to her with a straight face. "You could pick up a crate of diarrhea water and maybe some powder for bladder control, while you're at it."

Startled, Cooper looked up from the journal, then gave a low howl of laughter. Brant joined in with a deep rumble of his own.

Her vexation multiplied. These two men joked like adolescent schoolboys, for heaven's sake.

She eyed the dark sculpted face. And avoided looking directly at his mouth. "Have you got a health problem you'd like to tell us about, Brant?"

Instead of shutting it down, her comment ratcheted up the laughter.

She pressed the journal onto her lap, the pages shuffling against her long skirts. "You two are juvenile."

"You're the one who said it," Cooper reminded her.

She shook her head.

Cooper just couldn't hold his tongue. "Those two guns of his?" He motioned to Brant's heavy holsters. "Bought 'em off a man condemned to hang."

She frowned. "That's gruesome. I don't wish to hear it."

"But he saved him. Cut him down in the middle of the Rocky Mountains, just as the posse was about to kill him."

Victoria pressed the pages of the journal together and used it to fan her face. "That's wonderful," she said with frustration. She leaned over to the swooning medical student. "Perhaps if Mr. MacQuaid would grant you the time, you might ask for his autograph."

Cooper scowled, finally getting the message. No more stupid talk of hangings and guns.

She didn't know what Brant's reaction was,

for she didn't bother to look. She withdrew her needlepoint from her satchel and counted her stitches. One, two, three…

But she was still watching everything from the corner of her eye.

Brant moved his legs away from the younger man. He tried to get comfortable. He dug his spine into the seat and rearranged his broad shoulders in the tight space. That didn't seem to work, so he folded one muscled arm across his lap, then changed his mind and stretched it out across the back of the seat.

Ha, she thought with a smirk of pleasure. Let him be as uncomfortable as she was. Cooper seemed the only one who felt at home, sitting still for long periods of time. Of course, he was a much smaller man.

But she was tinier than Cooper, and she couldn't seem to find any comfort. She wiggled her bottom on the firm seat…pressed her elbow against the door…rearranged her shoulders….

"Uncomfortable?" Brant asked her with a subtle grin.

"Not at all. I was just thinking how luxurious this coach is, compared to the dog sleds I had to use this winter."

"You came all the way up here by sled?" asked Cooper.

"No, no. Around Skagway and Dyea."

"Ah." Cooper nodded.

Outside, Gus whistled at the horses. The team slowed down and the coach turned a sharp corner. Something didn't feel right, though. Her sense of balance was off. The coach was tilting too much. She grabbed the handle of the door by instinct. With a bang as loud as a clap of thunder, the floor beneath her gave way.

"Ahhh!"

The coach crashed to the ground on her end and rolled over. She hit the roof with a whack to her skull. Both men tumbled down the coach on top of her. Their bodies slammed together, carriage screeching, and her screams pierced the air.

They were being overtaken.

The horses dragged the overturned coach along the bumpy trail. Every hard jolt pounded up her spine. Gus was shouting something. In her haze she tried to make out the words.

"Whoa! Stop!"

Inside the coach, their limbs thrashed together. Cooper's weight fell on top of her, a medical bag knocked her arm, and Brant was pushed up against her, his face pressed against her nose.

With a panicked holler from Gus outside, the horses neighed and the coach slowed until it finally came to a shuddering stop.

She caught her breath. She ached all over.

No one moved.

Were the men hurt? With her heart drumming against her ribs, her cranium pounding with pain, and Brant's long limbs wrapped around her, she braced herself for what might come next. Thieves? Murderers?

Chapter Three

Twisted into a heap with the two others, Brant remained calm as he tried to figure out what happened. His forehead was pressed into the top corner of the overturned stagecoach, above the window, and Victoria was wrapped around his side. "Victoria? You all right?"

"Yeah," she moaned. "…someone…shooting at us…"

"No," Brant murmured in a reassuring voice. "No one's shooting at us. Cooper?"

Lying on top of Brant's back, fairly light even though his full weight was bearing down, Cooper stirred.

"Don't move too quickly." Brant steeled his shoulders to protect Cooper from sliding down farther and toppling over Victoria. "In case something's broken."

Cooper kneed Brant's leg as he squirmed to rise.

"Slower," Brant told him. He eased his arm out beneath the heavy crush of Victoria's bosom and shifted his thigh away from the bare warmth of hers.

She retaliated with an elbow to his ribs, and yanked hard to pull down her skirt hems from up around her waist.

Brant snatched his hat off her legs. Mighty fine curves encased in stockings.

"Our wheel broke off," he told them. He heard the gentle sound of hooves trampling grass. Gus must've unhitched the horses.

Cooper stopped shoving his arms and legs around, as if taking a moment to note they were lying on the right side of the coach. "What the hell are we riding in? Piece of dung."

"Get off me," Victoria hollered to the both of them when she seemed to realize no one was hurt.

Brant couldn't comply fast enough. In her own special way, she was revealing she wasn't hurt, either.

"You all right in there?" Gus hollered from above their heads, through the coach someplace.

Brant exhaled with relief at the sound of the old guy's voice. "We're fine. You okay?"

"Twisted my leg a bit."

"The horses?" Brant hoped they weren't injured.

"Just scared. I unhitched 'em."

The top door, now facing straight up at the sky, rattled a few times, then after a firm pull by Gus, creaked open. Sunlight blasted down on them.

Cooper's boot dug into Brant's spine as he climbed out. Brant couldn't see what was going on outside, but as Cooper hopped out, he must've toppled over Gus, for no one was there to help Victoria when she climbed on top of Brant's shoulder to exit.

Two men and they couldn't assist a lady?

"Let me help you," Brant told her, but he looked up in time to see the underpinnings of her thighs and pantaloons as she jumped out on her own, cowboy hat in hand.

He looked away in haste, trying not to emblazon that luscious eyeful in his memory.

She was so damn single-minded. When she'd been an adolescent, he hadn't noticed it much.

In a full-grown woman, it was annoying that she wouldn't allow him to help.

He rubbed the ache in his neck and rolled his sore shoulder, then eased his way upward through the makeshift tunnel and into a blast of bright warm air.

A hundred yards ahead, the two horses meandered through a clump of pines, still skittish as they nuzzled the air and each other.

When Brant leaped out onto the ground, his weight rocked the entire stagecoach behind him. He spotted Victoria. She was on her knees, already checking the driver's sore left ankle. The wide brim of her hat shielded her face. Gus was sitting on a pile of logs, hat removed, sweat staining his shirt.

Cooper stood by, watching with his hands shoved deep into his tweed pockets.

"Move it this way," she told Gus.

"Can't. It hurts."

"We need ice. Since we haven't got any, cold water will do."

"I'll get it!" Cooper raced to the twisted coach, his string tie blowing in the cool wind as he grabbed an empty pail that was tethered to the top.

He scrambled toward the rush of a creek behind the woods.

Brant took a look at the rutted road behind them, trying to reconstruct what had happened. Two rotted logs lay in the distance, cracked in half with one end pointing up. That was what they'd hit. The runaway iron wheel lay in the grass fifty feet beyond that. He took a stroll to examine its condition.

The pins had snapped. The rim and the sprockets, however, didn't look damaged. The coach had been in good condition when they'd left Skagway. He'd seen to it himself that the wheels had been greased and bolted. If it weren't for that log, the accident wouldn't have happened.

Brant would tend to the wheel later, after making sure Gus was okay.

Heading back, Brant hauled Victoria's medical bag out of the coach and walked over to her side.

Gus's sock was off and his ankle was as big as a turnip. Hell. Brant crouched down beside Victoria and planted her bag on the ground.

"Thanks," she said.

All he saw was her hat, bobbing up and down while she turned the injured ankle.

"Oww!" Gus hollered.

"Sorry. I have to test how far it can go to see if it's broken."

Gus yanked his foot away from her grasp. "It's not!"

He shooed her away with his crumpled hat, refusing to cooperate further.

She planted her hands on her lap and slid up to her feet. "Just twisted awful bad. It's best if we leave your boot on, as a natural splint. It'll control the swelling better than anything else. Put it back on while you still can. Leave the sock off." She gave it to him and Gus gingerly rocked it back onto his foot, the ankle already bigger than it was. "We'll pack a cold cloth down inside to help. Rest for a bit till we figure out how to get the coach turned over."

She bent over and firmly hauled Gus's leg up onto the logs to elevate it. Her slender hands held a lot of power. Matter of fact, thought Brant, the whole woman did.

Gus leaned back and peered at Cooper as he came running back with a full pail of water, barely able to balance the thing as it sloshed onto his boots.

Victoria was appreciative. She kneeled to her medicine bag and removed some linen strips, soaked them in the chilly water and packed them into Gus's boot. Cooper tried to help, but she already had it managed.

Gus looked over her shoulder to the horses.

"They're fine," Brant told him. "Got spooked real good."

"How's the coach?" Cooper looked up from his right hand, which he was gripping and squeezing repeatedly.

"Scratched," Brant told him. "Nothing broken."

Victoria focused on Cooper's hand. "What's wrong?"

"Just sore from haulin' water."

Was it? Brant stared as the young man rubbed

his wrist. It was the other hand he'd used to carry the pail.

Victoria turned around and from beneath the brim of her wide hat, she eyed the busted stagecoach. "The carriage—"

"Don't worry," Brant assured her. "I'll use a horse to raise it."

"But the broken wheel—"

"We snapped a pin. I'll take Gus's tools and try to hammer out another one."

"Well, you've thought of everything…." Her voice trailed off. The left side of her face, the part he could now see, looked ghostly pale. A ridge of sweat lined her upper lip. It seemed to him she was swaying.

He reached out and grabbed her left shoulder. Was she feeling shaky from the accident? He wheeled around to get a good look at her eyes.

His gut tightened with fear. She couldn't seem to focus.

"You sure you're all right?"

"Just…thirsty." She reached up to her cowboy hat, made an attempt to pull at the brim, but missed.

His sense of danger heightened as he tried to determine what was wrong.

She mumbled, drowsy. "Don't know how my head got wet… Must've been an open canteen in the coach…."

That's when her eyes flickered shut and she fainted. He leaped to catch her. Her hat fell off and his gut went cold.

The entire right side of her head was caked in blood.

Victoria drifted in and out of a haze. Pain in her head seared the top of her skull and worked its way downward to the base of her neck, where the muscles clenched. Colors of the ocean dazzled the back of her eyes as her mind flittered. Turquoise… emerald…deep mystifying blue…

She felt a cold cloth press against her temple. A sharp stab of pain ricocheted through her, and she winced.

"Sorry," a deep voice murmured. "Sorry…"

Another softer voice, a young man's, murmured, "Here's a clean one. I'll wash that one."

The pressure of the cloth didn't stop digging into her sore head.

She tried to swat the hand, but couldn't lift hers. She struggled to form words, opening her mouth to shout "Enough," but all she heard was the chirp of a chickadee and the rush of wind through faraway trees.

She was home again in St. Louis, lying at the base of the swing with the wind knocked out of her, gasping for air and clutching at her lungs, pain from the hard wooden swing pounding through her head where a lump the size of an apple had already formed.

"Victoria, what have you done?" came her mother's strained voice. "Why can't you sit still?"

"Please leave her be," Sarah had replied. "She's hurt. Are you all right, honey?"

"Up. Up before your father gets home."

"Brant will be here any minute, Victoria. Please get up."

"And the preacher," said their mother. "He won't like to see those skirts scuffed with dirt."

The cloth pressed at her head again, bringing her to the present. She swung to push it away, and this time a firm hand caught hers.

"I've gotta clean the blood. See how deep this thing is."

An older man spoke then. Gus? "Tryin' to help me, while the whole time she cracked her own skull. Poor little thing. Let's take her home."

Home. Where was home?

A bedroom she shared with her sister. Frilly with white lace curtains and fluffy pillows, where Sarah had confided her first kiss with her dreamy new beau…Brant in topcoat and tails arriving to take her to the Governor's Ball.

Victoria was out cold for four hours, and Brant's shoulders tensed tighter with every passing minute as he struggled to fix the wheel. When she finally stirred, Cooper was at her side while Brant and Gus were fastening a new pin to the coach, twenty yards away.

The whoop of Cooper's holler echoed through the air. "She's comin' to! She's comin' to!"

Brant dropped his hammer to the ground and raced to her side at the cottonwoods.

She rose up off the wool blankets, moaning in discomfort. A bandage was wrapped around her head, on the right side where the three-inch gash had produced all the blood. Stopped now, thank goodness, but it had given everyone a scare.

She fingered the bandages. "What am I... What happened?"

"You banged your head." Brant kneeled on the grass beside her. Cooper was on her other side. "On the ceiling of the coach. Remember? The accident?"

"Hmm..." Clutching her head, she fell back against the gray wool bedroll.

He held his breath.

Don't slip away again.

"Rest," Gus told her as he inched in close to the gnarled tree trunk. "Don't try to get up."

"You lost some blood," said Cooper. "You'll be light-headed."

She turned her face to the direction of the coach. "You pulled it to its feet."

Brant brought her a glass of water. She took the tin cup from him and their fingers brushed.

"We did all kinds of things while you were sleeping," said Cooper. "Fixed the wheel. Made grub. You hungry?"

"Thirsty." She drank weakly from the tin cup.

She was responding well to the questions, Brant noted. She understood where she was, and who they were. Her hair was disheveled, her face still pale and her lips cracked, but her eyes could focus.

"You better eat something," Gus told her, "so you're strong enough for us to head back."

"Head back?" Victoria pulled her covers to her chin and pushed herself up to a sitting position on the blankets. "I'm not going back."

"But your head," Cooper told her. "You lost consciousness. You were dizzy and disoriented. I think…I think…you've got a concussion."

"Oh." Befuddled, she blinked at the ground. "How long was I out?"

"Four hours and twenty minutes," Brant replied. The other two men looked at him in surprise. "Well, I couldn't help but notice the time."

She closed her eyes. He dipped forward.

Was he losing her?

"I'm taking you home."

Her lids snapped opened again. "No." She squinted in the brightness of the long afternoon sun. "People depend on me. Please…give me till the morning. If I'm well enough to go on, we go on. If not, I promise to obey."

He hesitated. He wanted to go on, too. Desperately in fact. He had a job to finish that no one here knew about—the real reason he'd maneuvered to become her bodyguard. But he wasn't about to sacrifice her health for his job.

"I vaguely remember knocking my head. Is the cut bad?"

"Quite a lot of surface bleeding," said Cooper. "Your hat soaked up most of it. That's why we didn't notice at first. Doesn't appear you cracked your skull."

She swallowed and paused for a moment. Then turned toward Cooper. "Thank you for the bandaging. I…I'm surprised, actually…I didn't think you… Well, in any case, thank you."

Cooper stared, expressionless, but a stain of crimson crept up his tender jaw. He peered over at Brant—they both knew the truth of who'd bandaged her head—but Cooper didn't say. At the sight of all that blood, the young man had been slow to jump in, but in the end, he had helped by giving Brant instructions.

It didn't matter, Brant thought. Only her recovery did.

Cooper pushed himself up off the ground to refill

her water. His injured wrist was wrapped with a cold linen compress to keep the swelling down.

All of them were injured except Brant.

She stared at him, moving back uneasily as if just noticing how close Brant was sitting. The awkward moment strained till he couldn't take it, so he, too, rose to his feet.

"Got a job to finish." He headed to the wheel.

Gus hobbled to the campfire and the boiling pot above it. "I'll get you a plate of beans. Good for your strength."

Brant heaved his shoulder against the wheel and tapped the hammer to the pin.

The ping, ping, ping rattled around him and amplified the turmoil he was struggling with.

What she didn't know—what he hadn't confessed—was he was still a bounty hunter.

Back in St. Louis, she hadn't respected him much in that line of work.

Here in Alaska, he was keeping it a secret. He was letting her believe he was working as a bodyguard, that he'd left his job as a bounty hunter behind.

Truth was, he was after Walker Dixon. A cold-blooded killer whose nickname was Charcoal because that's the condition he left his victims in after he robbed them and lit their homes on fire.

Dixon lived in the vicinity of Glitter Mountain,

but she likely didn't know anything about him, since Dixon didn't advertise his name or how many states he was wanted in for murder. He'd come to Alaska sometime last year, Brant figured, hiding like a coward in a pretty little valley whose entrance through a mountain pass was guarded night and day by his vigilante men.

A mountain pass Brant hadn't been able to penetrate on his own, as much as he'd been trying all summer long. But one he knew Victoria had breached in May.

Medical people were treated like royalty in this neck of the woods, by folks who knew who they were. As they should be. Even criminals wanted medical help on occasion and welcomed them through the area. As long as no one asked too much about them.

Had she ever treated Dixon as a patient? Brant rolled it over in his mind.

Dixon, apparently, wasn't stirring up trouble where he lived now. Not on the outside, anyway, so Victoria likely wouldn't suspect his criminal past. But Brant wondered if a thief and killer like that could ever turn the page on his past, no matter how hard he tried to live a cleaner life.

In the next week, Brant figured, Victoria would take Brant through the pass, then Brant would order the man they were supposed to meet, John Abraham, to whisk her and her team out of there, redirect them and take them home. Brant alone would take her medical supplies into Glitter Mountain for the injured gold miners, and take care of Dixon.

No one would ever be in danger except Brant.

No, sir, he thought as he shouldered the wheel, no need to tell her he was still a bounty hunter. If Victoria knew, she would surely object to providing cover for him on this journey, as he raced to capture Alaska's most notorious criminal.

If Brant confessed his plans to her, she'd tell Gus and Cooper. There was no telling what they'd do—try to help Brant, or try to convince him he was mistaken. Either way, Brant would have three of them to deal with then.

It was safer to divert them at the mountain pass and keep them out of it altogether.

He looked back to see Victoria sitting up against the trunk of the tree, spooning beans from her plate. Her bandage wobbled on her head. The fine features of her face contrasted to the thick wad of gauze.

A thread of guilt latched around him and squeezed.

Maybe he wouldn't have to make any difficult choices. Maybe tomorrow, she wouldn't be well enough to go on and he'd have to escort her home.

He was hoping for her good health, though. Good health for her sake, not his.

Not his, he thought as he looked away again, unable to face the soft turn of her cheek and the innocent tilt of her mouth. He wasn't using her.

He wasn't.

Chapter Four

"All women like to be pampered."

In the early morning sunshine, Victoria awoke with a start to the sound of Brant advising Cooper on the matter of women.

She was lying underneath a lean-to made of branches. The canopy shielded her from direct sunlight. Now that the end of summer was near, there were no longer any days where sunshine lasted nearly twenty-four hours. The sun rose shortly before six in the morning, and set sometime past eight in the evening. By the time winter came, though, there'd be nearly twenty-four hours of perpetual darkness. She still wasn't accustomed to that.

Covered in fox furs in the icy chill, Victoria

struggled to sit up on an elbow but stopped when her head throbbed. She touched her forehead. Still bandaged.

The men's voices carried from the campfire. She peered through the angles of branches and saw the men poking at the coals with sticks.

"Don't you suppose," said Cooper, "women aren't all the same? Take, for instance, my neighbor. Susanna Prentiss. Eyes as pretty as the color of the Atlantic, but she doesn't want anything to do with me. I've been trying for three years to pamper her, but she doesn't notice me much. 'Course, I'm away at college an awful lot, and I think that's what really upsets her."

"They like to pretend they're different." Brant moved his tall frame away from the flicker of fire. "But I've never met one who didn't like the extra attention. A compliment on her dress, on her ability to ride. And you pretty much have to tell her night and day how you feel about her. There's nothing women like to talk about more than your feelings."

Cooper squawked with laughter, his jacket bulging open to reveal his wrinkled white shirt and swinging string tie.

Victoria shook her head at the pale advice, but stopped when the movement made her head pound more.

There was silence, then Cooper's voice in her

direction. "Her blankets are moving. I think she's getting up."

The two men strode over to her lean-to. All she could see was Brant's big scuffed boots and Cooper's slender ones.

Brant crouched down beside her, his handsome face invading her pocket of air. He twisted about freely, his wide-eyed expression an indication that he'd slept well. Mornings suited him, she realized.

"How you feeling?" He peered at her bandages.

"Not so good."

"Your head hurt?"

She strained forward into sunshine and nodded, then frowned away from the sun.

"Can I get you anything?"

"Coffee would be nice." Then because she'd overheard the men's earlier conversation, she added, "But please don't go out of your way to pamper me."

Brant tilted his head, his cowboy hat shielding her from the hot rays. "Just having a little fun. Didn't mean you."

"Since we're talking about the sexes, why is it you men think every problem's solution is either fists or money?"

Cooper bent low and looked into her eyes. "Pupils dilating at the same time. Same size, too."

She flapped her hands at him, irritated that her comment was being ignored.

"What does that mean?" Brant asked Cooper.

"No internal head injury."

"Oh," said Brant. "Good."

"So far," Cooper added.

Victoria clicked her tongue. "Fists or money," she repeated.

"Because," said Brant, "those usually are the only two solutions to just about every problem."

Both men shrugged as if it was the most natural answer on earth. Brant pressed his large palm to his chest and added with a hint of a smile. "Please don't paint all of us men with the same brush." He turned to Cooper. "You getting that coffee?"

"I got it," Gus hollered from the fire, making his way over with a tin cup. He handed it to her. "How you feelin', Victoria?"

She was starting to feel like a little ground squirrel trapped in a hole, the way all three men were staring at her through the branches of the lean-to. "A little shaky. If I get up—"

"No," said Brant. "You sit right there till I say you can move."

"Why?"

"My orders," said Cooper. "I'll get you some breakfast and in the meantime, Brant's going to ask you some questions."

Victoria watched the young man shuffle away with Gus. She turned back to Brant, who was crouched at her side, his long legs jutting toward her, the width of his chest beneath his fringed suede jacket blocking out the horses hitched at the trees behind him somewhere.

"What questions?"

"We need to see how good your memory is. Cooper's book says memory is a good indication of the severity of your concussion. And since I'm the one who knows the most about your childhood, I volunteered."

"My childhood? Why is that necessary?" She clenched the muscles of her jaw with a new bout of pain.

"Checking for amnesia."

"That's ridiculous. Maybe the questions are an excuse for you…for you to…"

"What?"

"Get into my business."

His jaw tightened. "Then you tell me. How would you suggest we check on your level of alertness? How do we know if you're fit to go on?"

She slumped back against the bedroll. The furs settled in around her shoulders. He did have a point. "I was born in St. Louis. Lived near the Mississippi."

"What color was your porch painted?"

"It wasn't. It's made of stone."

"Okay, good. What's your mother's Christian name?"

Sometimes it hurt to think of home and the people she'd left behind. Parents who had never understood her. "Madeleine."

He frowned and shook his head sadly. "Uh-oh. It's Harriet."

"That's her middle name. She liked Harriet better, and used it all the time with her friends. But her legal papers always say Madeleine."

"Maybe I should ask a better question."

"Come on, Brant. You know I'm fine."

The tug in her voice was stronger than she'd intended. His gaze washed over her face, like a new tide searching to clear the sand, or searching to clear the air between them.

"Before I left St. Louis," he said softly, "when I came back the second time…"

She pulled her elbows to her sides and dropped her focus to the silver furs around her knees. He wasn't going to bring that up now, was he?

"You were changed," he pressed on. "Harder toward me."

"What does it matter how I felt then?"

"It matters because every time you look at me now I still see the hurt in your eyes."

She looked away toward the fire and the two men

cooking her breakfast, unwilling to let Brant read whatever emotions her eyes were betraying.

"Five years is a long time to go without being able to explain to someone—"

She cut him off. "You were changed, that's all. I saw it the moment you returned from your journey and stepped onto our porch to speak to Sarah."

He stopped talking and looked down to his fingers. What more could he offer in explanation than what she knew already? He'd spent a year going after the killer of his best friend, Travis Redwood, outsmarting the law and hauling the criminal back to justice, but at what cost to her sister and their families?

"The end justifies the means?" she asked.

"No." He shook his head for emphasis. "I brought an outlaw to justice and it was the single most rewarding thing I've ever done in my life."

Victoria blinked up at him, saw the firmness in his jaw, the blunt cut of his upper lip. "I thought Sarah would be your greatest reward."

"That's a child's dream, Victoria."

The comment stunned her. She would never understand this man. Would never have anything in common with him. Despite that they ate the same meals and were traveling the same road, they didn't share anything the least bit personal.

"I don't mean that in a cruel way," he said. "We

were all kids once. It's just…I grew up awful fast when I walked into the bank that morning and saw Travis gunned down in the back. He was trying to help a teller get away, and the son of a—"

He cut himself short. "Well, you know the rest."

Yes. He deserted them.

"The day I left, I heard you were waiting for the preacher to arrive. Everyone, including Sarah, thought he was coming to ask for your hand in marriage."

Her nostrils flared. Her eyes stung.

"What happened?" His voice was a deep throb.

So he hadn't heard? He was the only one on the face of the earth who didn't know of her humiliation?

"He never asked me to be his wife."

"Why?"

She'd never told anyone the real truth. Not a single soul. She'd made up other excuses, the reality too embarrassing to reveal. But for some reason, whether it was the look in Brant's eyes or the fact that they were thousands of miles away from home, the words tumbled out.

"Martin told me…I didn't lead a life of purpose."

A breath escaped him.

She gulped back the sting of that awful moment. "I guess you weren't the only one who thought I was a child."

She lowered her eyes again and drew circles on her knee with her fingertip.

The moment stretched and stretched and stretched and her eyes stung so badly she hoped with all her might he'd turn away and leave her before the tears spilled over.

He didn't leave, though. He placed two fingers overtop hers and pressed her hand gently.

Through misty eyes, she watched his fingers, the heat of his touch doing odd things to her stomach.

"You sure proved Martin Shaughnessy wrong. The folks you help on the trail are forever grateful."

"It didn't help my cause," she whispered. "He married Sarah two years ago."

Apparently shocked, Brant dropped his hand. It left a cold spot on hers.

"Yeah," she said, lifting her chin in indignation. "Martin married Sarah."

Brant's eyes widened. "That's why you came to Alaska."

She straightened her posture and shifted her weight. "No. I came because they needed me."

His dark penetrating eyes wouldn't let go. "And that's why you're so mad at me. If I had married Sarah, then Martin wouldn't have been able to."

He was wrong! She sat there, silently stewing when what she wanted to do was smack something.

The tense moment was interrupted by Cooper,

who burst back onto the scene with a platter of ham and powdered mashed potatoes. "Food's ready!"

Brant swung his long legs away from her and stood up, so she could only see the knees of his denims. "Victoria seems to be fine," he told Cooper. "She's thinking straight and I… We're going to Glitter Mountain. Prepare to leave within the hour."

With the pounding of his boots on firm soil, Brant left as abruptly as he'd come. She stared at the back of his worn soles, wondering why fate had brought them back together. When she'd left St. Louis, she thought she was leaving behind the three men who'd deserted her.

First, there'd been the Reverend Martin Shaughnessy. She'd believed with her whole heart that the man of God had found her delightful and irresistible.

Then her father, for deserting her in spirit, leaving her out of family discussions, so heavily disappointed at the preacher's rejection that he had barely talked to her after that. He'd shamed her so much with his disappointment that she'd turned from a flighty adolescent who'd been interested in dresses and cosmetics and ballroom dancing to a solitary young adult who took to reading.

And finally here was Brant MacQuaid, a man who would always be a deserter, whether it was her sister or another poor woman. He'd never remain steadfast or loyal to any cause but his own. Victoria had witnessed it firsthand in St. Louis, dragging out the whole business with her sister for a full year before he'd said what was on his mind.

He was the kind of man who kept things from people he loved. Or said he loved.

All they were to each other were painful blisters of the past. He'd have to deal with her for two more weeks and that was all, Brant told himself the rest of the day. No more dumb reminiscing about a history neither of them wanted to remember.

They made their way along the deep ruts of the trail and stopped whenever they spotted a cabin and someone who might need medical treatment. Brant was always at her side, trying to ignore her presence. But every time her skirts brushed past his pant legs, or he caught Cooper staring at her, love-struck, a sharp jolt hammered through Brant's rib cage.

She wore her cowboy hat, concealing the bandages from patients, but however she wanted to hide it, getting over a concussion didn't seem likely in a day.

And that was another damn reason he had to watch her closely.

Gus was still sore and limping awful bad, but Cooper's hand seemed much better.

"Howdy, gents." In the midafternoon, Victoria stepped out of the coach and faced two fishermen standing by a river's edge. The men were scruffy, unshaven and greasy.

Unexpectedly, they drew their guns.

Brant's muscles flexed. He stepped up slowly and calmly and shielded her from the men. "We come in peace. No need to draw your weapons."

"Oh, Miss Windhaven." One of the men scratched his forehead and smiled, revealing yellowed teeth. "I do recall. You visited us in the spring."

"That's right. This is Brant MacQuaid. Brant, meet Wayde Stanforth and his brother, Ernie. Cooper's in the coach and Gus is in the driver's seat."

The men nodded at each other.

"How's your health?" she asked them.

"I'm fine," hollered Ernie, the plumper one, his eyes moving back and forth to the fishing rods they'd propped in the reeds when they'd seen the coach approaching.

"I've got a tooth that's botherin' me," said Wayde. "Got anything to kill the pain? We ran outta whiskey last week."

"Let's have a look." Victoria stepped over to him. The wild grasses on the riverside went halfway up her skirt, the dried yellow reeds a stark contrast to her deep chestnut hair, Brant noted. He glanced away, irritated at himself every time he noticed anything feminine about her.

Or whenever he remembered that kiss. And he was remembering an awful lot lately.

Cooper came up slowly from behind, hands in his pocket.

She peered into the lower right back of Wayde's mouth. "The molar's rotten."

"Ernie tried to help me yank it out, but we can't get at it properly."

"Cooper, you've got the proper tools in your bag. First, some dental powder please and a brush."

Cooper laid his medical bag to rest and rummaged through it. He handed Wayde the toothbrush and the man went to the river to clean up. In the meantime, Cooper removed some fancy pliers. When he passed them to Victoria, she staggered on her feet.

Brant caught her beneath the elbow and lowered her to a log.

The fishermen grew concerned. "She all right?" asked Ernie.

"Bumped her head yesterday. A bit groggy." Brant turned to Cooper. "You can pull the tooth."

Wayde scoffed as he returned from the river's edge, wiping white foam from his chin. "The boy doesn't look like he's got the strength."

Cooper shied away and handed Brant the instrument.

Brant frowned. "I'm no doctor."

"It's easy," said Victoria. "Have Wayde lie down, get a good grip on the tooth and yank. I could do it and I'm smaller than Cooper."

"I'd prefer you, mister," Wayde said to Brant.

Brant muttered. He was hired to be a bodyguard, not a dentist.

Cooper shrugged at him.

With a groan, Brant went to the river and washed his hands. He came back, took the pliers, kneeled at Wayde's side, and followed Victoria's instructions.

The tooth was more stubborn than he thought. He dug his knee into the dirt beside the man's head and twisted the molar from side to side. Muscles up his forearm clenched and released when the tooth finally popped out.

Trouble was, it was bleeding like hell. Cooper handed Brant gauze packing, Victoria took out a small bottle of cognac, soaked some remaining strips and had Brant pack it in tight.

Wayde looked green at first, then his facial color picked up again when the cognac started to numb the pain.

Victoria's eyes were closed by this time, which worried Brant. "Hey." He gently nudged her boot. "Hey, you sleeping?"

"Hmm?" She opened her lids. Taking a look around, she seemed to realize where she was.

Brant left the two brothers in Cooper's care, much to the young man's dismay.

"Why don't you stay?" asked Cooper.

"You can manage," Brant told him. "And why don't you give this other fella, Ernie, a toothbrush of his own?"

Victoria regained her energy after a light rest, and they drove again for hours in the stagecoach.

Brant occupied his time looking out at the river, the twists and turns of the flowing water, and the seabirds. He saw diving gulls, scavenging magpies, ravens in the trees, sparrows and finches flitting around the coach. He even spotted two black-tailed deer rummaging for ripe berries when they stopped for dinner.

Victoria spotted them, too, for she stopped scrubbing out the skillet by the river and stood entranced as the healthy male jerked his head and antlers her way, then darted through the trees in a blink of an eye. She laughed then, turned and caught Brant's eye and they shared a warm second before she quickly turned away and refocused on her dishwashing.

The next group of four men they met were headed to the gold fields of northern Alaska. A new gold strike, they admitted slowly. "We're furniture makers from northern New York." All young and muscular men who carried their weapons on their hips with expertise, Brant noticed. They also handled their horses with the same distinction.

"Need medical assistance?" Victoria called.

They were either stunned to see a woman's face pop out of the stagecoach, or amazed that anyone with medical skills was this far out in the open valley.

"No, ma'am." The leader, a man in his thirties with a heavy mustache, glanced around at the others from atop his mount. "But we'd be mighty obliged for a bit of company."

Sitting across from Victoria, Brant twitched uneasily beneath the eager faces gawking at her. The lead man shifted his slimy stare from her face, over her bosom and straight down to her lap. If the coach wasn't blocking his view, Brant was sure the slimy devil would've loved a gander at her legs, too.

Brant placed his weight on the seat and dropped his wrists to be sure to allow a good view of his Colts. "We're in a rush. Another time."

With a tip of his hat to the men, Brant whistled to Gus to roll on.

To her annoyance, they hightailed it out of there.

"What are you doing? What's wrong with a bit of company?"

"Two of the men carried Navy Colts. One had a

rifle, a pistol and a dagger. And I saw two others nodding to a third in some sort of signal."

"What does that prove?"

"They're not furniture makers."

She was silent.

"I don't know what they are, but they don't work on fine carpentry."

She said no more.

When they settled for the night, Gus and Cooper took to one area of the campfire, so Brant was stuck with her on the other. He supposed that Cooper and Gus thought she needed a bodyguard more than they did. But honest to God, why did Brant have to get stuck with her all the time?

Past midnight, he rolled under his bedroll, dozing lightly, fully clothed except for his holster. The guns were too massive to sleep with on, but they were nice and handy by his head. He peered through slit lids at Victoria, who was turning in her sleep, adjusting her silvery furs beneath the light of the moon. Her hips rolled up as she turned, and her high-heeled boot revealed itself on one end.

God, she was all woman.

Determined to ignore her, he shut his eyes. As he did, a loud gunshot ripped through the air, making his heart lurch and his hands jump for his Colts.

Chapter Five

⟨ornament⟩

Victoria bolted out of bed at the blast, skirts askew, corset off beneath her blouse. The sound of men's voices, whooping and hollering from deep within the forest, set her pulse reeling. In her fear, the air seemed to grow as thick as molasses as she breathed it in.

Brant was already poised above her with his Colt drawn. He pulled her by the wrist toward the stagecoach, followed by Gus and Cooper.

"What is it?" she whispered.

"Strangers. Shh."

He pressed a finger to his lips and motioned for her to crouch low, behind the protection of the coach. The horses were hitched a hundred yards away, jittery at the noises but not spooked. Yet.

Brant tossed Gus a rifle from behind the driver's seat and told him to wait there to protect her and Cooper while Brant went to investigate.

Now she realized why he'd kept insisting they all sleep with their boots on.

Her heels dug into the moist grass, as soft as bread dough. Part of her bandaging hung at eye level, restricting her vision. She rocked back toward the wheel, a bit dizzy. Stabilizing herself, she rewrapped the loose end of gauze, thankful there was no fresh bleeding.

Her eyes were riveted on Brant's wide shoulders as he pressed forward into the brush, toward the noises of men carrying on along the trail. The moon was dim through the trees, but everything was quite visible.

She feared for Brant. She wanted to holler, "Wait, don't go," but realized he was being paid to protect her and the others.

Dark clothing flashed through the branches. Two young men on horseback. One hurled an empty whiskey bottle at a tree and it crashed on the trunk.

Marauding drunks?

Friends or foe? She stiffened as she waited and prayed Brant wouldn't come to any harm. He had his guns pointed in the men's direction, and it pleased her to know how capable he was with his weapons.

"He'll get us out of this," Cooper whispered with awe. "Just you watch."

Gus nudged him to keep quiet.

Maybe the two men would pass by on the trail and not even realize Brant and the others were here, thought Victoria. As the horses found their footing along the rocky trail, the drunks were almost by them when Brant lowered his guns. With relief, she slumped against the ground.

The danger was over.

But then one of the drunks aimed high at a tree. "Owl in sight," he hollered, then blasted.

The owl fluttered its wings and tore off into the sky. Brant stepped out and shouted, "Lower your weapons! You'll hurt someone!"

But then one of the drunks spun around, aimed and fired through the trees at Brant.

She screamed, Cooper jumped on top of her to protect her, Gus came out blasting with his rifle and Brant shot back at the drunk.

She couldn't see a thing, but heard the shouting.

"Son of a bitch," one of the men roared. "You shot his hand!"

More gunshots.

"Drop your weapons!" Brant shouted again.

Gus's boots pounded on the earth, limping on his left side, but all she heard was the galloping of horses as the drunks tore off.

Then silence. Cooper moved off her. She slowly rose and looked.

Both Brant and Gus were standing, guns pointed toward the empty trail, unharmed.

Her heart beat wildly. Blood rushed to her face and pounded through her muscles. She raced to Brant's side.

"You hit one?"

He strode out onto the trail and picked up a fallen gun. "Nicked his wrist."

"He'll need bandaging."

"Could've been worse."

Cooper peered into the stillness. Horse hooves pounded through the air, getting softer and softer.

"Should we move out?" Gus asked Brant.

"Damn right. When they sober up, they might come looking for us."

Two days passed with Victoria looking over her shoulder, waiting and tensing for an ambush. Every rustle in the bushes had her jumping. It didn't help that at times, she still felt groggy and nauseated as she recovered from her concussion.

She was leaning over the dinner fire, stirring a pot of beef jerky on one side, and a pot of dehydrated potatoes on the other, when the dizziness caught her again.

Brant was at her side in a flash. He grabbed

her wrist, took the spoon and steered her toward a boulder.

"How long has this been going on?"

She sat down. "Only for a moment. I felt a bit woozy...."

"I mean how many days? Hiding your condition won't help things."

"I'm not hiding."

He tilted his dark head in disapproval. "You have to ask for help when you need it. Otherwise, I'll turn this coach around right now and we can all—"

"All right, all right." She held her bandaged head as it throbbed.

His voice went soft. "Sit here and relax. I'll finish the meal."

And he did.

It was strange to sit there doing nothing in the middle of the woods while a man did the cooking.

A nearby stream gurgled and a gentle wind plucked yellow leaves off the trees and swirled them around her feet. She inhaled a deep breath of misty cool air, tinged with the scent of coming winter. Autumn never lasted long in Alaska. A few weeks at best between summer and the coming of snow. Winter would be here soon.

But the weather wasn't what held her attention tonight. Tonight, she was focused, despite her best efforts to ignore him, on the man preparing supper.

He looked striking in his dark Stetson. It framed the dark bend of his eyebrows, the piercing gaze of his gray eyes, and the curve of his firm lips as he poked at the red embers beneath the pots.

With his sleeves rolled up, his muscled forearms were glazed by firelight. A light matting of dark hair accentuated his masculinity; so, too, did the agile way he moved around the fire. Ease and strength emanated from the toned thighs and the broad chest that tapered into a narrow waist.

It was his face, though, that said the most about him. The turn of his roughly shaven cheek, the confident way he mastered the fire, the silent brooding reflected in his expression and the quick way he had of flicking his attention to the slightest rustle in the woods around him.

And he was never without his guns. His holster dipped and swayed with his movements. In fact, he moved as though the weight around his hips didn't even register.

The guns were a reminder of all he truly was. A gunman. Sure, he was on the right side of the law, as her bodyguard, but she wondered what more he wanted out of life.

How long could a man go from job to job, being hired for his agility with weapons and the strength of his fists?

And what about when he got older? What skills would he have then?

At least, she thought, he was no longer a bounty hunter. She'd heard horrible stories of what some of those men did for the sake of a rich reward, how they themselves sometimes broke laws in order to capture a criminal. Their motivation was questionable. Most did it for the money.

She shuddered and looked down at the tips of her boots. She was a healer, not a fighter. She supposed she should be grateful that there were men like him around to protect her when necessary so that she could go about her duties.

She just didn't have that much in common with him, as far as goals in life.

He chased trouble. She ran away from it.

He'd taken solitary jobs as a bodyguard, traipsing all over the country in the past few years, while she'd traveled to Alaska and was trying to establish a home. A life where she had friends and companions, and hopefully one day, a husband.

She'd met a few good men. Capable men who were eager to take up with her. Some, of course, were questionable characters, with shady backgrounds looking for anonymity here in Alaska. But others were decent, hardworking men with brothers and sisters and extended family.

She just hadn't found the right one yet.

"You hungry?" Brant hooked a towel around the handle of one pot and swung it to the rock beside her. The pot sizzled next to her.

Flustered at the way he was looking at her, she fanned her hands toward the fire.

"Umm-hmm," she said. "All this fresh air works up my appetite."

He smiled, and for the first time since they'd started out on this journey, she took the moment for what it was. Perhaps she was just too tired to fight him.

Or maybe, if only for tonight, she preferred to enjoy the soft sounds of the insects, the crackle of logs in the fire, the soothing tones of Gus and Cooper talking about folks they'd both left behind in Pennsylvania. Cooper in the big city of Philadelphia. Gus in the farmland, in the western part of the state.

When the meal was finished, their stomachs blissfully full and the coffee simmering softly on the iron grate of the fire, Brant removed his deck of cards.

"Again?" she asked. "Don't you ever tire of cribbage?"

"Tonight, you and I'll be partners."

The way he said partners made her shift uneasily. Partners in cards. She supposed she could handle that.

It was a new game he'd taught them two nights ago. She figured it was a way for him to keep an eye on her recovery, how sharp she was and whether she was slipping back into her concussion. She didn't mind going along with pretending she was unaware how closely he was watching her. Something about his interest was flattering.

Was she imagining his concern? His polite civility?

"Your turn," he said twenty minutes later when the four of them were seated on a thick wool blanket close to the fire.

She removed her jack of spades and added to the count. "Thirteen."

"Lucky thirteen," he whispered, and there it was. That extra little nod of attention, the quirk of his lips when he spoke to her, the tilt of dark hair that flicked on his forehead.

She wasn't imagining it. She felt the silent pull between them tonight, noticed his gentle ribbing of her card-playing ability. Or was it a gentle teasing of something more basic? This evening she felt more awkward than usual around him, more aware of how sloppy she must look with the bandage wrapped around her head.

"Thirty-one," announced Cooper with glee, adding two points to the peg board of the other team.

"Gotta catch up," Brant warned her. His eyes sparkled. There it was again.

She was being silly. She turned away in haste, but following the other's lead, added a winning card to the pile.

"The good guys win tonight," Brant teased.

"Aw, come on," muttered Gus. "Rematch."

"Nope, sorry," Brant insisted. "Maybe tomorrow night. What were the stakes again? I win your coach, Gus. And, Cooper, the pretty little lady wins your spiffy new medical bag and all your books."

Brant winked at Victoria. She smiled lightly at his joke. They weren't gambling for any stakes. It was just a friendly game of cards. But wouldn't it be nice to win all those books?

She studied Brant as he collected the cards and put away the crib board.

Charming, yes. Should she fall for his tricks? No.

She pushed herself up from the blanket and walked to the stagecoach, where she prepared for bed.

She stood outside the door, with her two large carpetbags within easy reach on the seats.

It didn't make sense to change into nightclothes out here in the open. When they stopped at an inn, she was perfectly safe, but here, with her being the only woman and those two drunk men still on the loose, she'd remain in her clothes. She did, however, pull out her blouse from the skirt's waistband, and loosen the chemise beneath. She'd already tugged off her corset when she'd cleaned up earlier tonight, and none of the men appeared to have noticed.

She pulled out a hand mirror. Maybe she'd tackle her bandage tonight. She hadn't yet had a good look at the cut herself, and if the wound began to fester, she'd need—

A crackle in the woods made her jump. She peered through the scraggly tree trunks toward the trail. No sign of any strangers. She stared for a moment longer through the hazy mix of moonlight and shadows. Nothing.

Every night since they'd met up with the two troublemaking men, Brant had insisted they camp well off the beaten track.

There was nothing out there.

She turned back to her bags and removed the blouse she intended to wear in the morning, along with fresh underclothes. On the journey she had to wear each item of clothing at least two or three days. Tomorrow was her day for freshening.

Another crack made her yelp. "Oh!"

"It's just me," said Brant behind the stagecoach. "Are you decent?"

She tugged at the end of her blouse and suddenly

self-conscious of her loosened clothing and lack of corset, pressed her arms up around her chest.

Brant came around the corner.

He lowered his gaze from her face to her chest, blinked and looked away. "I heard some noises."

"I heard them, too."

"No need to worry. Skunks are on the prowl fifty feet to the right." He pointed in that direction.

"Oh. Are they after our food?"

"It's all been put away."

She nodded. He glanced at the mirror she'd propped up on the window of the stagecoach, then down to the open medical bag with the fresh bandaging and bottle of cleansing tonic.

"Need some help?"

"I'd...I'd like to take a look at the gash."

"Might be a good idea."

It would be easier with a second set of hands. Someone to swab the area in places she couldn't see.

"Maybe I should call for Cooper."

"I'm a bit taller. Can see more without you having to squat to the mirror. And Cooper's already sleeping."

"Ah." She tried not to sound too disappointed, but she couldn't help but feel naked around him. She found the tucked end of the linen and unwrapped it from her head.

The crusty end stuck a bit to her hair.

He leaned in. "Just a minute. I got it."

But it was glued solid. He yanked a bit and she cried out, "Whoa."

"Sorry. Let me take some of this tonic and soak it."

She went to help him, but he seemed to know what he was doing. He soaked two wads of cotton with the tonic, then dabbed at her head. She winced at the sting.

"Sorry."

He continued. Within moments, the old crusted bandage gave way.

"Hmm," he murmured, studying the cut.

"Let me see."

"I wouldn't—"

Too late, she swung around to the hand mirror, had a look at the bloody mess and gasped. "Oh, God, it's infected."

"I don't think so. It's just all that old blood. Here, let me soak it off and you can see."

She stood perfectly still as he dabbed and cleansed and patiently went back and forth from the supplies to her scalp. With her head tilted toward his chest, she had a view of his thighs.

There was a ripple of muscles beneath his denim jeans as he moved gracefully around her. With the scent of this man so close to her nostrils, she realized she hadn't been this aware of Brant since she was fourteen and had seen him helping her father oil down a brand-new stagecoach he'd had delivered one hot summer. Brant had taken off his shirt in the blazing sun, his skin bronzed with color, his energy and skill rippling off his face as well as every muscle in his torso.

He dabbed her head one last time and the ache jolted her from her memories. She moaned softly and closed her eyes. When she opened them again, he was staring down at her.

"All finished." His voice was rough. His dark gaze teetered on her eyes, then slid down her face and lingered on her lips.

Gooseflesh prickled up her arms and along her spine. Her breasts felt heavy, her breathing clamped. She chided herself, ignored Brant and moved to the mirror.

Her brown hair was plastered with water and stained a strange pinkish color. The cut itself was two inches long, straight above the left side and buried in her hair. Thankfully, a huge healthy scab covered the gash. There was no redness, no pus, no infection.

She breathed a sigh of relief.

"I suppose," he said gently beside her ear, "I could've shaved the hair before I bandaged you, but I just wanted to stop the bleeding as fast as I could."

"You?" She whirled around. "You mean Cooper."

His lashes flickered. "Cooper." He nodded.

What did that mean? "Cooper cleaned me up, right?"

She could see it in his face. It wasn't Cooper. The young medical student had been as scared to touch her as he was everyone else. Why hadn't she known that?

Perhaps she had, somewhere deep down. But if she'd admitted to herself that it was Brant who'd bandaged her, it would have meant being beholden to a man she hadn't trusted with anything personal.

And yet, he'd done this kind thing.

The moment stretched. A sliver of golden light outlined the features of his face—the golden cheek, the bristly jaw, the rich mouth.

He must have felt the tug, too, for he pressed his hands to her shoulders, drew her close and kissed her full on the mouth.

Chapter Six

~~~~~~

Victoria was more woman than Brant expected.

Her warmth and softness nestled against his body, her full hips and the soft swell of her loose bosom pressed against his hard chest. He demanded her full attention with his kiss, and she responded with much more vigor and passion than he'd thought her capable.

Why hadn't he ever noticed her as a beautiful young woman back in St. Louis?

She was, wasn't she? Gorgeous and talented, and her body was every man's dream.

Her lips were soft and luscious, the taste of her breath sweet and mystifying and all things female. Her hands, coming up around his neck, urged him to press closer and so he did. He stepped inside the circle of her body, hip to hip. His rock-hard attraction would be very apparent, if she only shifted a few inches to her right. He groaned with the feeling of Victoria in his arms, pleasured at the scent of her skin, marveled at her silky smooth throat when he cupped his hand there.

She gave it all back to him. Every touch of his lips, the light pressure of his tongue, the easy stroke of his thumb down her jaw. She was here and she was with him.

He slipped his hand up along her waist, so eager to explore that which he had never been able to have. Indeed, that which he'd never even suspected was here—a smart, strong and capable woman in every regard.

When his hand reached the soft cup of her breast, she gasped into his mouth and pulled away.

"All right, all right," she said quietly. "I lost my head there for a minute, but what do you think you're…" Her sentence trailed off. "First a kiss, and then how much more? I'm grateful for your help with my injury, but this isn't how I show my gratitude."

Her words stung.

"You think I want repayment?"

"No. I just…I don't think of you in these… I want a man who…who'll stay put long enough…." Another sentence that went dead on her lips.

Long enough to what? Commit to a woman?

How the hell did she jump from a kiss to a future together?

Incredible!

Victoria didn't have to finish her words. He could see in the dampened, disappointed glimmer of those emerald green eyes.

"You think you can just waltz back into my life," she said softly, "that because we're so far away from St. Louis, I don't remember what kind of man you are?"

His jaw twitched.

He hadn't been good enough for her sister, so what made him think he was good enough for her?

"Ridiculous, isn't it?" he asked with a cold pang in the hollow of his chest. "We're two different types of people. And you're the kind that always thinks you're above mine."

She winced with that, but he didn't care.

"Did you ever think that maybe you and your sister weren't the right kind for me?"

Whatever acceptance he'd seen in her eyes minutes earlier vanished. Replaced with a stone-cold determination to keep the hell out of his way.

Good.

He grabbed his hat and headed back to the fire.

Victoria tossed on her side all night long, unable to drift to sleep because of the anger sizzling through her veins.

Who did he think he was, kissing her, then telling her off? Her dreams didn't help matters. She'd dreamt she and Brant were living in the same house, she as his servant and he ordering her about, night and day. In an awful twist of events, she'd come down the stairs one morning to discover his wife was her sister, Sarah.

Victoria had barely closed her eyes when she felt the sun's rays heating her face.

Someone nudged her boot.

"Wake up, Victoria."

She stirred and squinted in the sunshine. It was Gus.

"We gotta get movin'. Bags are packed, we're just waitin' on you."

"How's your ankle?"

"Better. Swellin's come down quite a bit."

"Keep it propped up on the driver's seat whenever you can, okay?"

He nodded and she scrambled to get up. She changed her blouse and brushed her teeth. She tucked her hat gingerly on her bare head, the scabbing much firmer than it was last night.

Gus had prepared a sandwich for her and she ate it on the stagecoach to save time.

Brant sat across from her, peering out the window and avoiding a glance in her direction for most of the morning.

That suited her just fine.

She pushed thoughts of Brant and last night's outrageously rude kiss far out of her head. And she managed to accomplish it, too, leafing through Cooper's journals and catching glimpses of redbirds and bluebirds through the bushes.

The path was getting less civilized. Trees occasionally scratched the side of the coach and sometimes Gus had to stop to think of how he'd turn the next gulley.

They'd make it, though, thought Victoria. They had in the spring and they would now. As long as there was no snow and ice. She tucked the collar of her duster closer to her throat to keep out the morning chill.

Cooper did most of the talking this morning. "Take a look here in the text. This new surgical technique recommends we suture the bladder separately to the wall of muscles—"

"Please," Brant interrupted. "Take it easy on the details. Save it for the operation."

Cooper turned to her. "They recommend two grains of muscle relaxant before the anesthetic is even administered."

"You're so good with the books," she said as kindly as she knew how. And so scared with actual patients.

Brant stared long and hard at the young man. "You said your father got you into medical school."

Cooper leafed through his pages. "That's right."

"If it had been your choice, what college would you have gone to?"

The comment flustered Cooper. He swatted at a fly and scratched his ear. "The Philadelphia School of Medicine is the most prestigious—"

"That's not what I asked."

Victoria shuffled her boots and shifted on the tight seat.

"I think I might've enjoyed accounting."

She leaned in, determined to give the lad some confidence. "You're exceptional with your physiology books, Cooper. You can memorize charts and diseases like no one I've ever met."

Brant shrugged with impatience. "But it's his father's call and not his."

"Cooper's done all the work in his first year, not his father. Cooper's getting ninety-five and ninety-eight percent on his exams."

"Oral or written?" asked Brant.

"Both," she replied proudly.

"See. That's what I mean." Brant leaned his bulging shoulder against the plank boards of the coach. "He hasn't been assessed yet, has he, when he's with actual patients?"

Cooper shrugged and looked down at his journal. Sunshine lit up the thin hairs on his upper lip.

Victoria frowned. "There's time for that. If Cooper truly wants to excel at being a physician, I can show him—"

"No, no, no. Brant's right." Cooper sucked in a deep breath and readjusted his pant leg. "I haven't decided yet if this is what I want to do."

Victoria sagged against her cushion. To have things all lined up, to have the chance to go to medical school and paid for—something she would have jumped on if circumstances had been different for her—was such a squander. How could Cooper not appreciate this astounding opportunity?

Brant's dark eyes glimmered in her direction. Was it a shimmer of victory?

The carriage came to a stop in a small clearing.

She threw open the door and bounced out, furious with Brant and not exactly sure why. She confronted him as he stepped out of the coach and stretched his long legs. The wind tugged at the hairs at his neck as he adjusted his Stetson.

She couldn't bite her words back any longer. "Why is it that you can so easily leave behind things that matter most?"

"You don't know what you're talking about."

"People. Family. A good future."

He grumbled something as she blurted what had

been burning on her tongue for five years. "Just because your father pushed you in a direction you didn't like, you left politics to spite him. But you have no right convincing this young man to leave medicine. No right whatsoever!"

Perhaps by the sting in his eyes, he finally came to realize how much he'd lost when he left St. Louis. With a huff of exclamation, she reeled away and left.

Brant was still fuming at Victoria's assumptions about him minutes later as they approached two men who were using tents for homes. Judging from the size of their clearing, the stack of chopped wood, the laundry line and the strewn household items, they'd been here a few months.

Brant had no intention of telling Cooper what to do. The kid had to decide. Not Brant. Not the kid's father.

Not even Victoria.

Couldn't she see that?

What right did she have to confuse the kid if he had no talent for medicine? Memorizing a bunch of words off a page, but scared stiff to go near a person.

What sort of talent was that?

It was not as if Cooper was as talented as Victoria.

He looked up at her. She'd slid into a conversation with these two old brothers, as smooth as apple pie with her friendly voice, her charming manner that made folks instantly drop their guard, and the mesmerizing way she had of making men of all ages stare at her beauty.

"Come closer. Haven't seen a woman in four months. Not since I stepped off the ship in Skagway."

"Well, sir, we come with good intentions. Are there any medical problems you're concerned with?"

The two old guys looked at each other, then back at her and Cooper.

"Nope," one finally said, shrugging.

"Are you sure, Mr. Finch?" She peered from one brother to the other.

Both men were dressed in overalls and both insisted on being called Mr. Finch. One had a beard. The other one was clean-shaven and looked younger.

Brant leaned against a tree, grateful to stretch his legs after being cramped up for three hours. He caught sight of several drying pelts, fox furs stretched over wooden frames. And a stack of deer pelts that must've been twenty deep.

Fur trappers. Very successful, at that.

One of the brothers, the older one with a gray beard, narrowed his eyes at Brant. In a silent gesture of friendliness, Brant put his hands in the air for a moment, indicating he had no interest in their furs.

The man relaxed and turned back to Victoria. "My brother broke his arm in the spring."

"It's healed on its own," his brother countered.

"But you're having problems—"

"I said it's fine."

Victoria stepped forward and placed her medical bag on the ground. "Perhaps the doctor here might have a look."

"That boy's a doctor?"

"Not yet, sir," Cooper began to explain in that roundabout way he had. "Not technically. I'm studying—"

"You," said the Finch brother with the broken arm, pointing to Victoria. "You can have a look at it if you stay for lunch. Haven't had the pleasure of a woman's company for a real long time. You remind me of my daughter."

Cooper smiled and stepped back. He'd gotten out of another commitment.

See? Brant silently asked Victoria. *The kid didn't even try to help.*

Victoria buttoned her lips and indicated they go sit on a couple of hand-carved chairs. Cooper followed but the elder Mr. Finch stopped him.

Brant, however, wasn't about to let her go

with two strange men alone, without his protection. When he followed, the clean-shaven brother attempted to stop him, but Brant raised his eyebrows in defiance, and the man relented.

Not so hard, when a person was persistent. That's all Cooper had to do. Be persistent and he'd be able to look at the broken arm, too.

"What happened to your head?" the younger brother with the smooth cheeks asked her.

"Bumped it in the coach." She tilted her head downward as she examined the lump on his forearm. The movement revealed her scab to him and his brother.

Since last night she'd washed away the last of the blood from her hair and pinned it up into a loose knot. Made her look a bit older, thought Brant.

Now she reminded him of his schoolteacher back in the third grade. A schoolteacher he'd had a crush on every time she bent over or reached high on the chalkboard and her blouse popped out of her skirt....

"Something wrong?" Victoria caught him staring.

"Huh? Oh...no." He looked away. "I was just interested in Mr. Finch's broken arm."

"How'd you break your ulna?" she asked.

"My what?"

"That's what this bone's called. The ulna."

"Dove after a rabbit that got away."

"It hasn't set properly," she told him.

"Tell me somethin' I don't know."

"We could… I could…" She stared up at the old man. "I could break the bone again and set it properly with a proper splint."

"See, I told ya," his brother piped up. "That's what we should've done. Broken it again. I told ya."

"Ah, hah," said the other one, yanking back his arm from her lap. "And I suppose as well as breakin' my ulna for the second time, you'd charge me for it, too?"

Brant stuck his tongue in the pocket of his cheek to hide his smile. Victoria caught it anyway and scowled at him.

She turned back to the man. "Nursing is how I make my living. But if you're unable to pay, I wouldn't leave you stranded. Of course I wouldn't charge you."

"He can pay," said Brant. "He's got a lot of valuable pelts out there."

The other brother, the older cheapskate, glared at him this time.

"No sense taking advantage of a lady," Brant explained. "So your answer's yes. She'll not only break your bone, she'll charge you the going rate."

The younger Mr. Finch rolled down his sleeve

over the warped arm. "As tempting as that offer sounds, I'll have to pass."

"Come on, Danny boy," his brother urged.

"No," the man replied. "Let her break your arm!"

"I'm not the one who can't sleep at night because of the ache."

"Only when it's raining."

"That ache might continue even if it's reset," Victoria said honestly.

Dead silence.

The elder Mr. Finch stood up. His baggy overalls were twice the size of his behind. "Can you at least give him something for the ache?"

"I've got some opiates—"

"Got any whiskey? Just plain, old-fashioned whiskey? We ran out two months ago."

"I think I've got an extra bottle or two."

They had a whole crate—twelve bottles—tied to the top of the stagecoach, thought Brant. He supposed she was being careful to make the crate last the whole trip.

"Okay, I'll buy the whiskey. But I'll pass on the bone-crackin'."

"You sure?" She smiled. "I'm pretty good at breaking arms."

She was kidding now, thought Brant. Teasing the two old guys. The younger Mr. Finch squinted at her beneath his mop of gray hair, not quite sure.

Then he chuckled. His brother followed in laughter, his gray beard bobbing and his legs rattling beneath his overalls as the group made their way back to the stagecoach.

She fixed them up with two bottles of high-grade, prairie-made whiskey.

They had a wonderful lunch of braised venison. She passed on the offer of a fur pelt as payment. Instead, the brothers paid her for the whiskey with a smoked hock, a stew of rabbit and pickled greens they'd bottled and made themselves earlier in the summer.

Food was much more valuable to Victoria. She already had enough pelts to keep her warm.

Wise woman, thought Brant.

The afternoon journey passed in relative silence. The population was getting sparser, with no cabins seen for hours. In fact, they didn't meet up with anyone else all day.

They found a quiet place by a riverbank that evening, when Brant's anger at her had long dissipated, replaced by the decision to let Cooper battle out his own future. He and Victoria could both do whatever they wanted. If the kid wanted to be pushed around by his father, or by Victoria, that was Cooper's damn problem.

Besides, Cooper could be easily wooed in any

direction by Victoria. Hell, she just had to sneeze and he ran to her side.

Look at them, thought Brant as he followed them down to the riverbank. He was still her bodyguard—their bodyguard—and it was his duty to offer protection night and day.

Victoria took the time to clean up at the river's edge, determined now to soap up her hair and wash it out well.

Cooper held the soap and the towels, mesmerized by the sway of her hair. Or maybe her hips. Or maybe the rest of her body that she'd unstrapped from her corset hours ago and allowed to bounce and move unencumbered. Not that either man noticed much.

Ha.

Brant stood behind her, letting her know he was here, too, in case Cooper left and she stripped naked to bathe or something.

Whoa, he thought. Where'd that come from?

Brant tried to shake the image of a naked Victoria out of his mind. What was with him this evening? Why was he so caught up in this situation?

More important, what could he do about the distraction? What he needed to do was let things evolve between Cooper and Victoria and stop noticing the details. That might sound like a fine plan of action, except that one of his strengths was noticing things most people didn't. Great for his line of work, not so great when he was trying to ignore everything about Victoria.

He inhaled deeply, ran his hands along his holster, pivoted away from the hair-washing and peered across the river. Something shiny glimmered for a second, then disappeared. Holding his breath, Brant didn't take his eyes off the spot.

Chapter Seven

"Down," Brant whispered fifty feet away from Victoria.

She had both hands locked into her hair, shampooing around her wound and laughing with Cooper, when she heard the call.

Her nerves jolted at Brant's harsh whisper. She swung around to look at him, soap and water swinging from the top of her head. Brant crouched into the reeds and signaled for both of them to get down.

By the cold look on his face, she knew there was trouble across the river.

Cooper grabbed her around the waist and dove into the grass behind a willow tree.

Her head remained a big ball of soap, but she wiped her wet fingers against the tall grasses. Sunlight slanted over the mountains, over the reeds, the bottom half of her skirt, and brushed against her petticoats. Cooper's breathing came harsh beside her ear, as her own pulse bounded in her throat.

She peered across the riverbank, over the swirling waters, through dozens of trees, and made out the shape of a man's cowboy hat. Then another one, the same tan color. When they turned toward her again, she knew by their height and shape who they were.

Her heart knocked against her ribs. The two marauding drunks. They were back, just as Brant predicted they'd be.

Her brain told her that logically, they could be back for any number of reasons. Maybe they were returning to wherever they'd come from in the first place. Maybe they were gold miners, panning the riverbeds for new veins.

Maybe, maybe, maybe.

But her heart pounded with the truth—they were back to gun down the man who'd shot them.

Brant.

He rolled down the slope of grass and came up beside her and Cooper. No one spoke, but Brant had his guns out and pointed them square across the water, waiting for any indication to shoot.

The men didn't seem to notice them. They were

busy making camp, unloading the saddlebags off their horses, then collecting firewood.

Minutes ticked by in agonizing slowness.

A couple of times, the men looked up over the water, as if staring straight at them, but Victoria, Cooper and Brant remained perfectly still in the reeds behind the cluster of trees.

When it was clear the men weren't coming after them, Brant signaled for her and Cooper to return to camp.

She clawed her way up the slope as though any squeak would bring a gun blast from the strangers. With her mouth as dry as a cotton rag, her muscles straining as hard as she could in a bent position, she raced for her life.

As soon as she made it to the top of the slope, hidden behind a line of trees, she straightened her spine and bolted toward their camp.

Panting, she yelled at Gus standing at the campfire. "Put out the fire! Put out the fire!"

He didn't ask any questions. He kicked dirt on the small flames he was starting, took the shovel next to him and completed the job.

Cooper came in behind her, running with the pot of rinse water he'd intended to wash her hair with. He poured it over the fire instead, but was quickly stopped by Gus.

"Too much steam and sizzle," Gus told him.

Brant went straight for the horses and started to hitch them to the stagecoach. "The drunks are across the river. They're making camp. We've got to move."

Victoria rinsed her hair with the warm water from the coffeepot, toweled up, and raced to collect the bedrolls and blankets they'd set up for sleeping. She shoved them into the coach, then dove in beside Cooper.

She shivered from the snap of cold hair on her shoulder. Gooseflesh crawled along her scalp.

Brant stayed outside in the driver's seat with Gus.

He guided the horses onto the tightening trail.

With the wind at their backs and the two men across the river still not showing their faces, the coach creaked out of the woods. They rumbled up speed.

Victoria clamped the loose wool blankets around her and pivoted to the small horizontal window behind her seat. Shivering now, unable to control the cold and the fear, she peered through the pane and searched the woods. Her gaze skimmed the campsite they were leaving behind and the bushes around it for any sign of the monsters. Her heart beat madly as she prayed for their safety.

Walker Dixon was the type of man who hated waiting. He hated waiting for the snow to come, he hated waiting for a woman to get ready for the evening, and right now, he hated waiting for medical help to arrive for his father.

He stormed out of his cabin. The structure sat on a slope on Glitter Mountain, overlooking the village of the same name. Dixon couldn't control the rage that boiled up within him. His massive legs pounded with each footstep, and his muscles clenched with the need to pounce on something. He spat out the matchstick he'd been chewing on, pulled out his revolver, and aimed it at the messenger who'd just arrived on horseback.

"Better be good news, Gutter."

In the intense morning sun, Gutter rubbed his bristly jaw and squirmed in the saddle. The brim of his broad black hat framed gritty cheeks and small dark eyes.

"Might not be exactly what you're expectin' to hear."

"Where's my nurse?" Dixon's broad back shook with the rage in his voice. Although he hadn't met the nurse last time she was through, she was supposed to be here the middle part of August. Hell, it was already the end of August.

"Likely got tied up on the trail. Mulroy and Thorpe are looking for 'em. I hear there might be a doctor with her this time."

"Then where the hell are they? My father's lyin' in there with a broken arm."

Gutter darted a nervous glance at the cabin. "Yes, sir. I…"

"He's burnin' with a fever this mornin' and I don't want to catch it!"

"Are you sure it's something you can catch? I mean, if it stems from his broken bone—"

Dixon raised his gun and the son of a bitch shut up.

"They'll come through," Gutter mumbled. He moved from side to side in the saddle, dark features slicked up from grime. "Mulroy and Thorpe always do."

Dixon took a cold hard look at the bearer of this bad news. Coldly, he aimed square between Gutter's eyes. Holding a gun on the man put steel in Dixon's spine when he saw the coward tremble.

"You're the one who suggested they go, Gutter. If they're not here by tomorrow, I'll pull this sweet trigger."

"If…if I could drum up a doctor from thin air, you know I would."

"Send out two more men to look for 'em. Now!"

Gutter's chest jerked with his breathing. "Right away, sir."

He backed up his horse slowly, eyes on Dixon's weapon, bowed his head in deference and tore off for their other cabin at the opening of the clearing, to get two more men.

What had Dixon done by coming here to Alaska? He slowly lowered his gun, while the thoughts inside his head wouldn't leave him alone.

This land was supposed to protect him—and his father and his men—till the law grew weary of chasin' him and just let him be.

Dammit. He dropped his head. Just let him be.

He was tired of runnin'. Tired of it all.

His pa was one of the miners who'd staked the first claim in Glitter Mountain. But other stupid men had created a weak tunnel that couldn't support its own weight. When the tunnel had collapsed on his pa, Dixon shot the three men responsible for the cave-in. It had only given him a moment's pleasure. Until he'd seen how badly injured his pa was. A broken arm to a man of sixty wasn't easy to mend. And now the wound was festering.

At the twitter of morning birds, Dixon turned his head to the right. Beyond the edge of the cliff, through the trees below, the cabins of Glitter Mountain shimmered in the morning light. Most leaves had fallen from the branches, and the mass of color on the ground ranged from yellow to red. The other trees, the ones with needles, remained green and bushy and blocked most of his view.

He inhaled the earthy fragrance of Alaska. At

one time, he'd loved these smells. Mosses and ferns, and fresh air melted right off the glaciers.

The reason he'd been drawn to settle here last year was because the village looked like a slice of heaven, that part of Oregon where he'd grown up. The place where his pa, one of the greatest bank robbers California had ever seen, had shown him how to shoot his first man. Where Dixon had bedded his first whore.

Now this place had turned into a slice of hell—a town filled with poison that had failed to produce any decent amount of gold and was threatening to take the life of his father. It was the town itself. Dixon felt the ominous vibration in his bones.

The whole town was evil and so was everything in it.

One of his ladies came running up the hill. Maria. Twentysomething, chunky curves and a mouth that did wonders for a man. "Dixon! Dixon!"

She was sweaty from running. And still wearing the black lace blouse he'd half-ripped off her shoulders last night. Hell. Couldn't she take care of herself a little more?

"Yeah?"

"It's…it's my brother," she panted. "His broken foot… He woke up with a fever this morning."

"Shit." Out of four injured miners, her brother

and his pa were the only miners who'd survived the cave-in.

"Dixon, you gotta help! Get some medicine—"

Alarmed that she was coming closer, Dixon lifted his gun at her and stopped her cold. "Stay the hell away from me." He didn't want any fever contaminating *him*. And now she was just as putrid as her brother.

"But last night, you told me—"

He cocked the hammer. The charcoal cosmetics she used to stain her eyes were smeared from sleep. When her lids opened wide in alarm, she looked like a big bug staring at him.

Evil.

Only one thing he could do.

She must have sensed he was about to fire, for she dove and rolled into the bushes. He pulled the trigger, missed and cursed.

Chasing after her, he raced to the edge of the cliff. Thirty feet below his pointed boots, in the forested gully, her skirts flew through the trees. He aimed again, but it was hard to see her flying through the woods. He fired, but the skirts kept going.

Dammit.

He lowered his gun. Two bullets were enough to waste on a whore. He'd save the next ones for Mulroy and Thorpe.

* * *

"Heave!" Brant pressed his shoulder to the back of the stagecoach that was stuck in the mud, and called again to Gus at the front, and Cooper and Victoria beside Brant at the back. "Heave!"

It had been almost twenty-four hours since they'd escaped from those two men on the trail, but Lord only knew if they'd meet up again. It was up to Brant to get them out of this dire situation. As it were, they were sitting ducks.

The coach budged a couple of inches, then rolled back.

Exasperated, Brant stood up, pulled at his leather gloves and muttered a few choice words beneath his breath. "This crate's not going anywhere. Gus, unhitch the horses. We're moving out by saddle."

"We can't leave the coach here. Someone'll steal it. And then I'll be responsible."

"What do you suggest? Want to stay behind and guard it?"

"No. Let's just…" The old man slid off his seat, careful of the ankle that was still stiff and healing. He came around to join the other three.

"Let the horses rest for twenty minutes, and we'll try again."

Brant looked to Victoria. He could see the disappointment in her eyes, too. Cooper looked at the sunken wheels and rubbed his neck in despair.

"We've been at it for three hours already," Brant reminded Gus. "Hitching and unhitching them. Who knows where those men are behind us. We've got no time left."

Brant had tried shoveling out the mud, but it just kept coming. He'd tried piling branches into the softness to give the wheels some traction. That hadn't worked, either. What he needed was another two horses to pull harder.

Gus shook his gray head. He scratched his whiskers. "I'm not gonna leave the coach behind. It'll take me six months' salary to replace it."

"It might still be here when we swing back."

Gus scoffed. "Not likely. I'm also responsible for the horses, and you can't have those, either."

Brant planted his dirty gloved hands on his hips. "Well, I'm responsible for everyone's safety. Including yours. And safety trumps your coach."

Brant refused to keep arguing. He strode to the horses himself and unhitched one. With a groan of complaint, Gus came up beside him to take the other mare.

Brant knew the old man was on his side. He'd come around and help as best he could.

"Don't suppose you brought saddles?" Brant nudged him.

"No," said Gus. "But I've got blankets we can use."

"I'll ride with Victoria. You take Cooper."

"Gee, thanks. Nothin' I'd like better than to cozy up to another man."

"All right, you take—"

"Stop your arguing, both of you." Victoria was bent over her luggage that they'd tossed onto the grass, and was thinning it out. "I'll ride with Cooper and you two can ride together."

Brant frowned. "One heavy person has to ride with one lighter person."

Cooper bent over the bottles of whiskey in the crate and removed a few. "I'll ride with Victoria. Brant can—"

Brant wheeled around. "I've been hired to bring the whole lot of you to safety. Can't you just follow my advice for one moment and pipe down? We'll flip a coin."

"Heads, I choose," yelled Victoria.

He groaned. Why didn't she and the rest of them leave things up to him?

He brought his horse around to the back of the coach in order to start packing their gear into saddlebags, then looked down at the wheels anchored in the mud.

Hmm. That was different. The mud was drying around the wheels.

Maybe he could…

He left the horse and walked fifteen paces behind the coach.

With a huge burst of energy, he ran toward it and rammed it with his shoulder. It gave way. Six inches, then another six.

"Look!" Cooper called, then came the sounds of everyone running, clomping in wet muck.

They pushed and yanked and kicked that damn thing till the crate nearly ran over Gus, who'd picked up the frame at the front.

Three more feet and the damn thing was out.

Victoria's laughter started first. Her delight rolled through the air, followed by Cooper's. He'd fallen to the grass, spent by the excitement. Gus at the front hollered in a large whoop, and Brant grinned so wide it nearly hurt his face.

They didn't hear the men behind them until their guns clicked.

Brant whipped around. His hands flew to his holster.

Too late. The two drunks who'd shot up the trail three days ago had their weapons drawn and pointed.

Brant froze.

Their eyes were bloodshot, but focused. They—and their wrinkled clothes—reeked of whiskey. The short dark one had his wrist bandaged with a kerchief, so he was holding his gun in his left hand. Was he as good with his left as he'd been with his right?

His partner, a tall scruffy man with red hair, pointed his gun at Brant.

Were they here for him? Looking for revenge?

Eye to eye with the barrel of an Enfield revolver, Brant didn't move. But he assessed the situation. If they'd wanted to, they could've shot him already. They looked past him, as if not recognizing him from the other night. Had they been so liquored up then that they couldn't identify him now?

Didn't they recall the owl, the yelling and cursing, and Brant drawing his gun?

It appeared not.

The scruffy one turned his gun on Gus, who was half hidden at the front of the coach. "Drop the rifle, old-timer. Unless you'd like a gut full of bullets."

Gus did as he was asked and slowly came around to stand beside Victoria. He limped slightly, and the laces on his left boot were undone.

The coach rolled softly back into the mud, sinking into the exact rut it was stuck in before.

Brant winced. All that hard work for nothing.

The wounded man chuckled. "Don't worry. You won't be going anywhere soon in that thing."

The other gunman moved his six-shooter from person to person. "We've been trailing you for days. We hear one of you's a doctor. The young one, they said."

So that was what they wanted, thought Brant. They wanted medical skills.

The gunman's barrel stopped at Cooper, who turned as pale as a weak moon. "You."

Chapter Eight

Victoria slowly raised her hands in the air, trembling at what was happening. She looked to Brant's grim face, but he shook his head ever so slightly, silently telling her not to move.

Cooper stood frozen in the yellow grass, hands clenched in the air, posture stiff, mouth shaking. He told the men, "I can't help you."

"Sure ya can." The taller assailant used his gun to point to the bags.

They both smelled like alcohol, Victoria observed, but seemed coherent. It wouldn't be easy to overtake them. And if they were still liquored up, they were more apt to shoot sporadically.

She released a breath and tried to get her runaway pulse to simmer down.

"What do you want?" Brant asked the culprits. Brant took a step toward Cooper in an unspoken gesture of protection.

"Stay where you are, mister. Hate to shoot you dead."

Brant's mouth steeled into a grim line. Victoria caught the implication, too. Why wouldn't the men want them dead? Weren't they here to harm them? Avenge their injury?

Didn't they realize that Brant was responsible for the bloody wrist?

"We're here for the doctor. And your medicine. Everyone else can continue to Glitter Mountain. Or turn around and go home."

Victoria blinked as the news sank in. She was grateful they didn't realize her group was responsible for the gunman's injury, but they couldn't take Cooper.

"How do you know where we're headed?" asked Brant.

"Asked the folks on the trail behind you. You left a few satisfied customers."

"Then help us," said Brant. "Help us get there."

The two gunmen snickered. "We came for the doctor." The tall redheaded one pointed his gun at the luggage. "Pack your supplies. You got stuff for broken bones?"

"Our aim is to help everyone." Victoria inched

forward. "There's no need to do this. We're here on a medical mission. We'll bring medicine and see to your friends, if you'll just tell us where—"

"Shut up. We don't take orders from a woman. Dixon would kill us if you talked us into something he don't want."

Dixon? Their leader? She peered over at Brant, but he was already watching her reaction.

"Well, the first thing you're gonna do," said the man with the injured wrist, motioning to Cooper, "is take a look at my wrist. Bring over some clean bandages."

Cooper nodded weakly.

"Where you headed?" Brant stepped in front of Cooper, shielding him.

"You ask a lotta questions for a man standin' in front of a trigger."

The scruffy one walked over to Cooper and placed the tip of the barrel on Cooper's temple. Cooper's nostrils flared. He winced. "Get movin'," the man snarled.

Victoria started. "He doesn't—" Then she said, "Just take the medicine. And the splints. That's all you need. Leave him alone."

"You must be the nurse."

The men contemplated her. A river of contempt washed through her.

Again, without being seen by anyone but her, Brant shook his head softly.

Don't talk, he seemed to say.

"We should take her, too." The man looked at her with a threatening sneer. "A few things I'd like to do to her."

His partner stopped him. "He'll hang you upside down if we take one extra minute gettin' there."

Victoria wondered who he was. Who had sent them? This Dixon man?

The shorter man with the newly bandaged wrist looked to Cooper as he stepped back, finished wrapping. "Doctor's all we need." He kicked Cooper's bag. "Pack!"

Cooper's face twisted in fear. He bent down and collected his things. He took his duffel bag, shiny leather medical bag and, with a painful look of apology to Victoria, the medical crate that contained most of their stock supplies. The one she depended on for treating folks on the trail. Her stomach squeezed with a different sort of fear.

In a sudden move, Gus stepped forward to block them from taking Cooper.

The uninjured gunman whirled with fury, kicked Gus in his sore leg so hard Gus fell with a thump to the ground. Gus hollered with pain.

"Hey!" Brant's angry voice rumbled through the woods.

Victoria raced toward Gus the same time Brant did, but the gunmen stopped him.

"Not another step or I swear I'll shoot," the injured one told him, taking aim.

Brant groaned behind her as she looked at Gus's pale face. "You all right?"

Gus muttered beneath his breath and sat up. He leaned over to have a look at his ankle.

The rest happened very quickly. The men took one of the horses from the stagecoach, tied Cooper's bags to it, and forced him to ride at gunpoint. Then as they galloped away, they pointed their guns at Brant and Gus and Victoria.

Soon, the pounding beat of their horses' hooves echoed softer and softer through the trees as they sped away.

Her chest tightened till she could barely breathe. They'd taken Cooper. Dear young Cooper who couldn't stomach the sight of anything cruel.

How would he survive?

When the gunmen turned the last corner at the clump of pine trees, Brant raced to Gus's side. "You all right?"

Victoria dropped to her knees beside the old man, on the other side of him, facing Brant. Her face was still pale and her pulse still throbbing in her throat. Likely as fast as his own, thought Brant.

"Gus, can you move?" Brant asked.

The old guy moaned and managed to twist his foot.

Victoria shook her head as she examined the ankle. "They kicked you pretty hard. Left a boot mark."

"Son of a bitch," Gus muttered.

In one easy move, Brant slid his hand behind the old man's back and helped him to his feet. The old man wobbled, tried to plant his weight on his left foot, but couldn't do it.

He cursed. "What about the coach?" he asked. "If we could haul it back out of the mud, I could ride it."

"We'll never catch up to them in a coach," said Brant.

"Right." Gus nodded his head. "I think you better go without me."

"We can't do that," said Victoria.

Brant weighed their options.

"Go without me," Gus repeated.

"We can't leave you here," said Victoria.

"We've only got one horse, and even if we get the stagecoach pulled out of the mud, one horse can't get far pulling it."

"He's right," said Brant. "I'll go alone."

"No," said Victoria. "I won't be stuck here in the middle of nowhere."

"You two ride," Gus offered. "Find Cooper. I'll walk back to the Finch brothers."

"It'll take you forever. Maybe a full day."

"Got nothin' else to do." He shrugged. "I'll take it slow. I'll rest up here till my ankle feels better. Then I'll see if the brothers will come back to help me out of the mud."

Victoria leaned back on her haunches.

"It's a good plan," said Brant. "Maybe you should go with him."

"But I'm the one who knows something about medicine," she told him. "You don't. What if…if they beat up Cooper? What about the rest of those folks in Glitter Mountain who need medicine?"

Gus leaned back against the coach. "They won't harm Cooper till after they're done with him. Don't worry about that."

Brant frowned. "John Abraham's supposed to be meeting us somewhere near the mountain pass. He's good with his gun and we can join forces."

"They think we're stuck in the mud and can't go anywhere. They're not expecting us to chase after them on horseback. But it might dawn on them. They're not stupid." Victoria bent down on one knee, rifling through her bags, collecting her things. She tossed out extra skirts, an extra pair of boots and her medical texts. "We'll hide these on the stagecoach, and with any luck, they'll still be here when we come back."

If they made it back this way, thought Brant, but he didn't voice it.

She looked to Brant but neither said the awful words aloud.

"They mentioned Glitter Mountain," he said. "I think they're headed to the same place we are."

"And whoever's giving them orders needs medical help fast."

"Why would they let us go?" Gus asked. "Doesn't make sense. Why didn't they shoot us and just take Cooper?" He glanced at Victoria. "Sorry for bein' so blunt."

"Because they need us," said Victoria.

"Yeah," Brant agreed. He secured a blanket over the back of his mare. "They need us to go on with our intention to help the rest of the village. They don't want it getting back to Skagway that they shot the nurse. Lawmen would come after them, and no nurse would be likely to visit Glitter Mountain again. Or, more likely, they figure we're so scared now we'll just turn around and go back to Skagway."

Brant struggled with what he should tell Victoria and Gus. "Listen. These are dangerous men we're going after. Victoria, I don't know about your coming with me. If you stay with Gus, you could reach the Finch brothers and borrow their horses to get back to Skagway."

"No." Victoria's voice was firm. "You're hired to protect us as a bodyguard. And I'm not going back without Cooper. Who's to say it's safer going back than going forward? If I go back without you, I'll be lacking a bodyguard. Skagway's several days away. Glitter Mountain's only two. And the more time we waste talking about it, the farther away Cooper's getting."

Brant was in a bad spot. He was her bodyguard and fully intended on keeping it that way.

Cooper had been kidnapped and they only had one horse between them. That changed everything.

Brant would be damned if he let the young man slip away. If he and Victoria caught up with Cooper before the pass, Brant would turn around and head back to Skagway. He'd drop the others to safety, then rearm and get the help of as many men as he could to go after Dixon.

Or Brant might leave her in the capable hands of John Abraham, as originally planned, and go in alone.

"One more thing." Brant took a deep breath as he tied a skillet to his saddlebag. "There's a man they mentioned…an outlaw. Walker Dixon."

He wanted her to know the full extent of what she might be riding into.

Tying up her saddlebag, Victoria shook off the name. Gus didn't appear to recognize it, either.

"That's the leader they're talking about," she said.

"He's a cruel—" Brant stopped himself from swearing and wiped his mouth with the back of his hand. "Comes from Oregon, originally. Likes to burn down homes with people still in 'em. I hear he might be hiding out in Glitter Mountain."

Victoria shuddered. "When I was there in the spring," she said, "I met most of the village. Don't recall any Walker Dixon. Don't recall anyone dangerous. Just a handful of men. Couple of saloon girls. Fur trappers. A few speculative miners up the river."

"Dixon might be going by a different name."

"I still don't see how me and Gus going back to Skagway alone is any safer than heading out with you. These kind of men riddle the trails in both directions."

Brant nodded. "I can't argue that point. But I'll take you only if you promise to follow my orders."

She stared him in the eye for a moment, then her shoulders dipped slightly as she relented. "You're the bodyguard."

A pang of guilt nipped at his conscience, for not telling her he was after Walker Dixon. But on the other hand, Brant had told her exactly who Walker

Dixon was, and he wasn't hiding anything from her in terms of safety.

She threw her extra clothes into the stagecoach, raced to give Gus a hug, then mounted the mare. Brant swung up behind her on the blanket, easing his legs in behind hers.

"You sure you'll be okay, Gus?" she asked.

Gus scoffed. "I've been on my own, young lady, while you were still in cloth diapers. I've been stuck in worse spots. Shot in the chest once and left for dead. There's no one after me now. I'll find myself a nice walking stick and take it slowly. Got plenty of water in my canteen and time on my hands."

To prove it, he drew in a deep breath and bore his weight on his sore foot. This time, his facial expression didn't change.

"See? Better already."

Brant admired him for his strength.

The old guy looked toward the trees in the direction where young Cooper had disappeared. The woods were quiet, as if even the animals and birds knew enough to hide. "You get that boy back, you hear?"

Perched on top of the mare, Brant bent over to give the man a firm handshake. He squeezed the brim of his hat in a fond goodbye, dug his heels into the horse and they tore off.

* * *

An hour later, Brant and Victoria were racing through the trees, ducking branches, veering around bends, and sailing over gullies.

He sat behind her on the mare and inhaled the cool scent of her skin. The leather string of her cowboy hat was looped around her neck, while the hat itself lay across her chest, flopping up and down in time to the horse.

She surprised him. He admired her more than he cared to admit. How could the preacher have given up her? She was strong and graceful and relentless in her loyalty to Cooper.

Brant had nothing to feel guilty about. He was no longer hiding the danger that lay ahead. A danger, it might seem, that may be looming larger than Brant had anticipated. Even if he'd told her right off when they'd first set out from Skagway, nothing would've changed on their journey.

She'd been to Glitter Mountain this spring and nothing bad had happened to her.

Even criminals welcomed doctors and nurses.

Yet, Brant hadn't come clean about everything.

That he was still a bounty hunter, still racing across the country in pursuit of vicious criminals, still, God help him, enjoying the thrill of the chase and a job well done.

All the things she disapproved of.

He wasn't sure why her opinion weighed so much.

Maybe because she was a part of his past, his home life in St. Louis. Maybe her rejection of him symbolized how his family felt. People whose opinions mattered to him more than he'd ever thought possible at this stage in his life. He'd thought that he'd left those matters behind, that their turning their backs on him no longer made a difference.

Meeting up with Victoria and getting that ache in his chest every time he looked into her face proved just how much it all still hurt.

It hurt, too, to physically ride this close to her. She was drawn up in his arms, her skirts billowing out from either leg as she pressed her thighs to hold on tight. As he caught sight of the turn of her legs, the pretty knees, he imagined how those thighs would feel wrapped around him and riding him just as hard....

He shook his head to snap out of it.

He had no right to imagine her unclothed, beautiful, bareback and calling out his name.

There was a steep slope ahead. He slowed the mare to a trot.

For a brief moment, Victoria pressed heavily against his chest. It was comforting to hold her. To feel the sweet part of home, to protect that which he cherished, to remember what he'd suppressed for five long years.

The smell of hay in the autumn. The lively calls of train conductors at the station on a busy summer night. Knocking on Victoria's front door in preparation to meet Sarah, but always delighted to find Victoria there, as well. She, asking questions on where Sarah and Brant were going that evening, smiling shyly up at Brant, accepting the occasional mint or cinnamon stick he happened to bring by for the women of the house.

Then there was the memory of just days ago when he'd first set eyes on Victoria after all the time that had drifted between them, and being astonished at the beautiful turn of her cheek and the way the sun hit her mouth when she turned her head.

God help him. What was he doing here with her?

He would only suffer more heartache when she'd turn him away for the second time, and disappointment in himself that he hadn't been able to become the man her family had so craved for her sister. A man of gentle means, upstanding in the community and one whom they'd be proud to call son-in-law.

He pulled his torso away from her, so that cool air filled the space between them.

Gently, he nudged the mare down the vines of the deep gulch, through the shallow riverbed of gravel, and up again on the other slope. So very careful to keep his distance from Victoria. So very determined to erase all thoughts of home.

Chapter Nine

The two of them were alone. No Gus. No Cooper. Just Victoria and Brant. Under any other circumstance, she knew it would be considered brazen of her to travel with a man alone. But this was duty. And he was her paid bodyguard.

She turned her thoughts to more immediate concerns.

They'd been searching for Cooper all afternoon and evening. There was no sign of him nor his two captors, and she was getting frantic. Now as they prepared for sleep, the campfire swooshed and popped in front of her and Brant. He rolled out his bedroll, head to head with hers, while she watched from beside the creek.

"You think Gus is all right?" she asked.

"Absolutely. He knows this part of the country. He's good with a rifle. And right now he's probably telling the Finch brothers a story or two to keep 'em amused."

"I hope so." Then she thought again of Cooper. "How could they have vanished?" She walked to the boulders that circled the fire. "Are you sure they took this trail?"

"You saw the tracks."

He stood up and poked at the flames. The red tinge of firelight danced across the planes of his face. Dark stubble lined his jaw. "Three men on horseback. Their prints were slightly dry. That means they passed here a few hours ago."

"It could've been a different three riders."

"Not likely."

"Maybe we should keep riding till we catch up. Forgo sleep."

"You can barely sit up on the horse, you're so tired. Look at you."

"I can handle it."

She slumped onto the boulders, cozy and warm from the heat of the fire. She heard a small splash in the creek behind her and turned on the boulder to look.

Two geese squawked and flapped their wings. It was a pretty sight, so she turned her back to the fire and sat facing the water instead. The heat of the flames soaked into her backside and mellowed the sore muscles she'd gotten from riding.

"You'll be able to handle things even better with a good night's sleep."

"When did you learn to be so calm?"

He sat down beside her. His large cowboy boots dug into the earth.

"I used to be rash? Is that what you're telling me?"

"You could never wait for anything, as I recall. A new horse. A social party. Even when you went to search for Travis's killer—"

She stopped herself from finishing. Maybe it wasn't fair, or the right time, to talk about his old friend.

She stole a glance at his face.

From behind him, firelight lit up the wide expanse of his back and shoulders, so his face was in shadow. He'd long ago tossed his cowboy hat, and now his dark hair framed his firm temples and the rigid crease of his forehead.

Still, as she grew accustomed to the half darkness, she noticed the fine creases at his eyes and the slight tug that lifted the corner of his lips. They were lines of distinction, age and experience.

Very attractive.

She glanced away, determined not to think of him in those terms.

"Ah, Travis." Brant smiled at the mention of his friend, surprising her. "You never had a chance to meet him. But if you'd wanted to meet someone impatient, you only had to shake his hand. He'd no sooner arrive at a social, he'd want to be introduced to all the pretty ladies. And you, my dear, would be at the top of his list."

It was a disarming thing to say. Kind and generous. It brought a wisp of tenderness to her mouth.

The memory of his friend obviously brought back a good feeling in Brant.

Her next question was out before she could stop herself.

"What happened to you, Brant? What happened to your carefree outlook on life?"

He turned to face her, his muscled arm brushing her shoulder. The contact sent a tingle of perception racing through her.

"What do you mean?" His deep rich voice echoed over the gurgling water.

She inhaled the smell of burning wood, the hint of cedar shrubs around them, and the scent of his leather vest. She treaded lightly, although she had a sense that they were spiritually connected tonight, that she could ask him anything and he'd answer.

"I mean you're not the man Sarah fell in love with."

His eyes glimmered and he looked away at the mention of Sarah.

Her stomach flipped over. Perhaps he wouldn't answer anything she asked.

She gave him time.

His features mellowed. He watched the geese float by, then after a few moments, picked up a rock and skimmed it across the river.

"Sarah never knew me."

"You courted her for three years."

"Some people can know each other for decades and still not truly understand one another."

"Sarah spent every waking minute with either you or your mother. When you went searching for the man who shot Travis, she stopped going to social events. She wanted to wait till you got back."

"Maybe she shouldn't have waited."

Victoria stared at the silhouette of his dark cheek. A dimple flicked at the crease of his mouth. The air grew still. Or maybe it was just that the air rushing in and out of her lungs seemed trapped inside of her.

He watched the geese for a little while, and she was lulled into a trance beside him, feeling warm and reflective and enjoying this evening.

"Sarah married someone else quite easily. Didn't she?"

Victoria tilted her head. Her hair fell against her breast. "True enough."

He paused for a very long time as his gaze roved down her face. His upper lip tightened, his jawline clenched.

Her stomach screeched in silence.

He hadn't known the truth about Sarah remarrying until she'd told him. How disappointed was he that Sarah had married Martin?

Brant obviously still had feelings for something about his relationship with her sister, otherwise he wouldn't be staring at her like this.

"Did her marriage hurt you for long?" His voice was gentle, but nonetheless tugged at her painful memories, and increased the intimacy with Brant. They were speaking about such personal things. A month ago, she never would've thought it possible that she'd be seeing Brant again after all these years, let alone disclosing things she never confessed to anyone.

Should she say more? Should she confide in him totally? The news she had to give would only hurt him. The words simply wouldn't come out. Her chest tightened, her stomach clamped, her mouth grew dry.

"What is it?" he asked. He pulled at her hand in

a gesture of impatience, gently ribbing her. "What else have you got on your mind, Victoria? You can tell me. I can take it."

She wasn't sure she could take it. Not again. The same old rehashing of the same old story.

"What, Victoria?"

She clenched her hands in her lap. "They have two children. Twins. A boy and girl."

His intake of breath was audible.

She fought the sick feeling in her throat, the embarrassing knot stuck there like a big wad of cotton so she couldn't speak above it. How many nights had she lain awake, dreaming of life with Martin, hoping to have his children? Then guilt set in for thinking less of her sister for having the honor. Victoria loved her sister, wished her only the best. She didn't truly love Martin anymore.

She didn't. The realization struck her with a blow as sharp as the stone Brant had skimmed across the water.

How odd that she'd realize it now.

Maybe it was the distance separating them that had softened the blow of being rejected by the minister. Or maybe she'd grown in her own life, realizing the man had been an ass to say what he'd said to her all those years ago, about not being good enough for him.

She was enough. She was enough for herself, and she was pleased the way her life had turned out.

At least, in the general sense.

Her eyes lost their sting, her breathing rate slowed. She listened to the echo of the wind and the flapping of wings in the trees around them as the tension left her chest.

Brant didn't say a word, but he lay one of his large hands over hers and looked down into her eyes. Gently, up came his other hand to her face. His touch was warm and unexpected. It sent tingles up her skin.

His eyelids flickered, he pressed his lips together, and for a long stunned moment, she was sure he was going to kiss her.

Her arms felt heavy and she swore every place he touched her was on fire. She was ready this time.

But he didn't kiss her.

He rose and walked to the edge of the river, looking out upon the water as it gurgled and churned above the ancient rocks.

The heat of the fire seared her back. How strong the heat had grown in the minutes they'd been seated here together, and she hadn't noticed till now. She let the heat soak into her bones, unable to move for how inexplicably disappointed she was that he'd left her side.

Alone again. Wasn't she always?

* * *

It was getting a hell of a lot harder for Brant to be alone with Victoria. Her admission to him last night about the minister and Sarah having kids still had him thinking as he rose the next morning.

Victoria had been so awfully disappointed in disclosing it. It hadn't shocked Brant, though, if that was the reaction she'd expected to see. Once he'd discovered they were married, he knew children would only be a matter of time.

He changed his shirt behind the mare, and for a fleeting moment, Victoria looked up from brushing her hair and saw him in his sleeveless undershirt. The moment seemed to embarrass them both.

It was much more intimate than he'd intended, dressing in front of her and watching her pull her hairbrush through her long hair. Their moment seemed more like that of two lovers, or perhaps husband and wife, than stiff acquaintances who knew each other from a forgettable past.

Trapped was how he felt. Wasn't it?

Trapped by a woman who made invisible demands on him. She might not know it, and he doubted she was doing it on purpose, but dammit, just her physical presence and the way he was forced to notice she was a woman made him resent her. He didn't need her personal stories about the minister to upset him. Why should he care that Sarah had married Martin?

Why did Victoria care if he was upset?

Who the hell gave a damn about any of it?

He finished dressing.

Ten minutes later, appearing just as eager to get going as he, Victoria threw the mare's blanket over her back and patted it in place.

She fussed with her clothes, adjusting the waistband and fighting with her collar. She was obviously ill at ease. Funny how a night of sleep and daylight had completely changed the mood from last night.

Dammit, he'd wanted her. He'd wanted to kiss her silly. He'd wanted to tear off her clothes and crawl into bed with her, to kiss her all over and claim her as his own.

With a groan of pent-up frustration, he looked away and stepped up to the mare to give Victoria a boost.

Their conversation turned to the young medical student again, a topic that made Brant much more comfortable.

Chasing criminals was something Brant was good at, unlike his experiences with women. Sure, a fellow got lonely on the trail and he'd had his share of one-time encounters, but having to live with a woman day in and day out was above his…his…

Hell, he just wasn't suited.

"Cooper doesn't have much physical strength to fend off anyone." She planted her boot inside the palm of his outstretched hand and swung up onto the horse.

Her petticoats and the heel of her slender boot brushed his sleeve. He muttered and tried to look away from the view of her pretty ankles and calves. "He'll have to use his brains, then. He's got plenty of those."

She nodded repeatedly, as if trying to reassure herself. He mounted the horse, sliding in behind Victoria, and they headed off into the morning sun.

Hours passed while they rode as quickly as they could. Brush dragged across their heels, rocky soil had to be navigated slowly, and they gave the horse a chance to rest periodically. They ate in silence and thought in silence.

Good.

The afternoon turned to evening. Brant was still on high alert, tracking signs of the three men ahead of them.

The woods were quiet today.

At least on the outside.

They rode up the gentle slope of a mountain, then along a dry creek bed. Their serene physical surroundings were a complete contrast to what was still tormenting him on the inside. Victoria and her ability to heat him up without even being aware of the effect she was having on him. Just the scent of her hair and the feel of her waist aroused him.

With a groan, he shifted on the mare, trying to stretch away from Victoria.

The earth swelled and rolled beneath them as they plodded along, and the last of the trees fell behind as they headed into grasslands.

But there was the ever-constant presence of her shoulders and the back of her neck as he gripped the reins around her and cocooned her in the crook of his arms.

He shifted on the mare and tried holding the reins with only his right hand. It worked and he was able to avoid touching her, until the path got more rocky and he needed to hang on with both hands again.

He had no idea what she was thinking as the sleeve of his coat rubbed against her upper arms, but she cleared her throat and her spine stiffened.

"Still haven't caught up to him," she said softly.

"They're three riders with three horses. We're moving slower because our horse has a heavier load, and we have to stop to give her more time to rest."

They reached the top of a crest. A new vista greeted them in the valley below. He stopped for a moment as they admired the view.

The valley stretched for miles. A log cabin puffed out smoke on the side of the next mountain.

People. Thank God, people.

Brant kicked his heels into the mare and they rode faster. When they turned the final corner and heard the faint sound of voices, he slowed down. They inched closer until they stopped to view the sight before them.

A group of small children transformed the landscape.

Victoria moaned slightly. For a minute he thought she'd been hurt, but when he helped her off the horse, he could see she was transfixed by the sight of youngsters playing and calling to each other in the field. How long had it been since either Victoria or Brant had seen the delightful sight of children?

Did her mood mellow, too? Could he forget about his tense feelings for her as they visited with this family?

And better still, maybe these children and their folks had news of Cooper.

Chapter Ten

Standing in the tall grass between Brant and the shoulders of their horse, Victoria stood transfixed at the sight of the children. She soaked in the squeals of laughter, the chiding, the coaxing and pleading of the younger ones, the hollering and whistling of the older.

Two barefoot boys, roughly eight, squatted in the reeds, reminding Victoria of sandpipers at a water's edge. Three older boys in knickers and suspenders chased each other up a willow tree. A fourth adolescent was carving something into the trunk of a cedar. Three younger girls and a toddler were screaming in delight while another boy chased them with a rubber ball. And the two youngest girls, one who could barely walk, and, from the look of her,

her twin sister, waddled out of the reeds holding a collection of sticks.

Victoria giggled. Thirteen children. How many families did they belong to?

It was marvelous to watch them.

Brant seemed taken by it, too. When she recovered slightly and pivoted to see where he'd gone, she found him standing right at her elbow, smiling as the two girls in cloth diapers set down their pile of sticks, tried to balance themselves, but promptly fell over into the soft grasses.

Victoria and Brant let out a ripple of laughter at the same time. The mare reacted to the noise, nickered, stomped forward, and startled a couple of the children.

It started a reaction in the youthful group. Dirty faces snapped in their direction. The older ones frowned and raced to protect the younger ones. The toddlers with sticks whimpered and pointed.

Victoria's smile faded quickly, realizing they'd been frightened.

"It's all right." She stepped forward slowly, appealing to them with open hands. "We're friendly. We only came to say hello."

"Hello, ma'am." The oldest boy, who'd been carving into the tree, inched over. "Mister."

"Howdy," said Brant, not making any quick movements but holding out his hand to shake. "I'm

Brant MacQuaid. This here is Miss Victoria Windhaven."

"I'm Rusty."

"Pleased to meet you, Rusty."

The rest of the children, quiet as mice who'd been
uncovered in the reeds, looked up to their eldest
brother as if seeking permission to bolt. But at their
brother's hesitant and calm response, they stood
where they were.

"Are your folks around?" Victoria asked.

"Yes, ma'am. At the house. This way."

The boy still carried his knife unsheathed, she
noted.

Friendly but careful. A good way to be in the
middle of nowhere.

Victoria and Brant followed behind Rusty,
through the reeds on the gentle slope of the moun-
tainside, over a ditch and through a cluster of
woods.

Brant led the mare by the reins while the children
raced around them, staying twenty feet away. Victoria wished they'd come closer so she could perhaps lift one of the smaller ones, but they all kept
their distance.

"Mama, Mama!" a younger girl called at the
cabin as it came into view.

"Pa!" shouted one of the older boys.

Some held hands and ran at breakneck speed,

although that wasn't very fast, considering how short their little legs were.

"I found 'em," said one of the boys, nodding at Victoria and Brant as if he'd found an interesting pair of marbles.

"No, I saw 'em first!"

"I get to ask 'em about their horse."

"No, me!"

A younger girl playfully shoved her sister toward Victoria. "Touch the lady's hair," the girl said to her sister.

But before the sister could respond, another voice shrieked from behind and Victoria spun around to look.

"No," wailed the toddler, who was now being carried by an older brother. "Me touch!"

The brothers and sisters laughed at the outrage on the toddler's face, and pretty soon Victoria and Brant and the children were laughing. Victoria moved closer and allowed the youngster to pat her hair. Two of the girls joined in.

It felt like a circus, Victoria and Brant the circus animals who were surrounded by the children— their trainers—being led somewhere to perform for their parents.

The trees opened up and the rest of the huge log cabin fell into view.

"Mama, Mama, we brought you some people!"

"Pa!"

The place sat with a full view of the glorious river valley below. Mountains rose to the left and right, high pinnacles with tips coated in white sugar. Around them, autumn leaves were shedding. Clusters of yellow, red and orange dotted the landscape.

Even the evening sky, as dark as it was, looked beautifully ominous. Thunderous purple clouds scooped the air and created layers of dark and light. It looked like a postcard from heaven. Perhaps Michelangelo's clouds on the Sistine chapel, which Victoria had once seen in a textbook.

"Gonna rain," said Brant as he approached the man who came dashing out from behind the cabin, firewood in his arms.

The stranger set down the wood, signaled to someone else behind the cabin, and out came a woman in a soiled apron, holding dry laundry. A child's nightshirt.

They didn't smile immediately, but came forward for introductions.

Brant explained who they were, a nurse and bodyguard traveling through the district.

The folks relaxed and shook hands. They introduced themselves as Alberta and Zachary Ford.

Zachary's rubber boots were coated with mud. He kicked at the bark scraps by his feet. "Haven't seen any strangers here for six months. And today, we've already seen five."

"Five?" Brant reeled back in surprise.

Victoria's stomach tensed in anticipation of who the other visitors had been. She looked to Alberta for clues.

Alberta was rosy-cheeked and had the broad hands and thick forearms of a woman who was used to working hard. Her expression didn't give away anything, though.

"Yup." The man rubbed his neck. "Three men passed through about…oh, eight hours ago."

"A younger man with a medical bag?" Victoria asked, her pulse tripping all over itself.

"Yeah. Said his name was Cooper."

Every sinew of muscle seemed to twist in Victoria's chest. "Did he look…" She fingered the loose strands of hair at her temple. "Was he all right?"

"Yes, miss."

Victoria rubbed her forehead in relief.

Zachary added, "The other two men told me he was a doctor. Didn't talk much."

Brant explained how they'd been robbed by these men, and Cooper taken against his will.

"Good grief." Zachary's bristled cheeks thinned. "We had no idea."

"I knew it," said Alberta. "I told you those other men were no good."

"You did no such thing."

"Remember? When they said the younger children talked too much? I said they were no good."

"No good," mimicked a toddler in the background.

"And when they complained about the temperature of the coffee, honest to God, I wanted to throttle that ungrateful man. I'd been cooking breakfast for over an hour already, and they ride in and expect me to just drop everything—"

"No sense makin' a fuss now." Her husband shrugged away her complaints. "Let's offer these kind folks a cup of coffee."

Victoria eyed Brant. "No, thank you kindly," she said. "We really don't want you to go to any trouble."

"No trouble at all." The wife beamed broadly. Her smile was genuine. "My children have taken to you. They aren't often this quiet. And anyone whose company my children adore, I invite into my home."

"Very kind of you." Victoria followed her into the cabin, a little queasy at causing any potential arguments, a little afraid of what she'd learn about Cooper, and terribly disappointed that she and Brant were eight hours behind the other men.

That meant the men had ridden through the night and there was no telling when, or if, they'd ever catch up to Cooper. With thunderclouds on the horizon, if it rained, it would be difficult to make the mare carry her and Brant without risking injury to both man and beast.

They'd have to settle here till the storm passed.

"The children aren't all mine," Alberta told Victoria an hour later as they sat around the kitchen table, finishing up a generous meal of rabbit stew. "My sister and her husband headed to the coast last week to pick up supplies. We go in the spring, they go in the fall. Three of the children are theirs. Those boys, there, with the blackest hair." She pointed to three playing marbles against the wall. "They took their youngest two babies with them."

"Your children are very bright." Victoria found an extra hairbrush in her bag and gave it to one of the youngest girls.

Her chubby cheeks dimpled. She grasped it with delight and began brushing her rag doll's hair. Her sisters squeezed around to help.

Victoria eyed her medical bag on the far counter. "Have you had any illness in the home?"

"Not now, thank the Lord." Alberta knocked on the wooden table for good luck, then glanced at the last of her coffee and paused. "I lost my first two children to tuberculosis. Along with my first husband. Wasn't much older than you. Zachary, here, promised me a better life in Idaho. When the gold rush hit, we packed our kids and took off. Been fairly lucky at finding a few nuggets." Alberta's cheeks colored and she was suddenly flustered, perhaps at admitting so much to Victoria. "Don't tell no one."

Victoria shook her head. She wouldn't. She was touched that Alberta had confided in her.

They were interrupted by a pelting sound on the roof.

Alberta craned her head upward at the rafters. "Rain's here."

Victoria was grateful that their mare was already safe inside Zachary's roughly hewn barn, along with his mule and two other horses.

Brant and Zachary stopped their conversation at the far end of the table to listen to the deepening sounds on the roof.

The children squealed with delight and ran to the windows to look outside. Alberta rose from her chair, walked over to one of the square panes and squeezed her broad hips next to the youngest. She twisted her body to peer up at the sky. "It'll be washing down in sheets any minute. We best get you to the other cabin."

"Are you sure your sister won't mind?"

"Na," said Zachary.

Alberta agreed. "She'll be happy someone's stok-

ing her fire and keeping the spiders from building cobwebs. Come. I'll give you fresh sheets. The
cabin's not as big as this one, but it's got a separate
bedroom. Your bodyguard can sleep on the sofa."

"Thank you," Brant told them, rising to his full
height. Wherever they went, he seemed to fill a
room with the breadth of his shoulders.

Two of the girls came forward without being
asked, and helped collect towels and supplies for
Victoria.

Victoria looked down at the sheets and hoped her
embarrassment wasn't showing. She didn't look at
either Alberta, or Brant, who'd come over to carry
the gear. She felt her cheeks flush at the thought that
she'd be spending the night alone with him again,
and this time there'd be two witnesses.

Or rather, fifteen.

The sleeping arrangements weren't so shocking
when it was just between her and Brant, but it was
a quiet struggle to defend her propriety in front of
Alberta.

However, Alberta wasn't questioning Victoria's
virtue in any way. In fact, the woman acted as if it
was the most natural thing in the world.

Of course, having traveled to the Klondike
herself, Alberta would be well aware of how few
women had made it here, and how manners and
customs in the lower states, in the civilized world,

meant little in the middle of the wilderness. Folks did the best they could to survive.

Social rules were the first thing discarded in times of necessity.

Brant was her bodyguard, and where else would a bodyguard sleep but at the side of the person he was protecting? And having been robbed at gunpoint and her companion snatched, Victoria was given extra immunity against society's rules tonight.

The sound of rain grew harder against the roof.

"Hurry, now." Alberta rushed behind them.

Victoria placed her long leather duster over her shoulders and wedged her cowboy hat over her head.

After a quick good-night to all, she made a mad dash for the cabin on the far slope, yelping as the cold rain hit her face. She balled her shoulders tighter and braced her body against the assault.

Brant strode beside her, lugging their bags and huddling around her to shield her as best he could from the rain.

When they reached the door of the cabin and pushed it open, the downpour danced wildly on the roof, clicking and pinging. It was exhilarating to be nestled inside the comfort of a shelter, even if the room was stone-cold.

"Let's get this fire going." Brant tossed off his

wet jacket, and in a surprising move, scooped hers off her shoulder and hung it on a peg by the door.

She added her hat to the pile.

Water ran off their jackets and hit the floor. A mesmerizing, yet simple sound of beauty.

"They won't be going anywhere," Brant told her as he arranged the dry firewood in the fireplace. "Cooper and the thugs, I mean. Not in this weather."

"That's true," Victoria replied, her tension suddenly easing up. "God, that is so true." She kneeled beside him on the floor and helped him with the firewood. "That fact might be the only thing that keeps me from going mad about this whole situation. They're eight hours ahead of us, Brant."

"I know. But only because they missed a night of sleep. Sooner or later, it'll catch up to them." He shoved kindling into the lower part of the pile. "Did you hear what Zachary said?"

"What?"

"When he asked where Cooper was headed, he said Glitter Mountain."

"Yeah…" She didn't understand what Brant was getting at. "That's where we've been headed all along."

"But the two thugs with him—Mulroy and Thorpe, according to Zachary—didn't argue. So that means they are headed there. We were just guessing before."

"That's right." She nodded, pleased at how much of this puzzle they were able to piece together. "Alberta says Cooper looked scared and kept to himself, but she didn't see any…welts on Cooper's body or signs of harm."

Brant lit a match from the top of the fireplace, got the fire going, and turned to look at her. "You were real worried about that. I'm sorry."

She peered over at his solemn face and the seam of concentration running along his forehead, and wondered why he was apologizing.

"I'm sorry because it was my job to take care of all of you, and…" He gulped and looked back to the fire. "And I lost Cooper."

"Not for long," she whispered beside him. "Not for long."

It struck her for the first time how hard Brant was taking this. It wasn't just that they'd lost Cooper; it was a matter of honor for Brant, and genuine concern.

She slid closer on the rug they were kneeling on and put her hand on his arm, surprised at how hot and alive his body felt beneath her touch. He spun around, his warm breath grazing her cheek. Her lungs stopped moving.

Lord help her, she was alone with Brant.

Chapter Eleven

While they knelt side by side, Victoria looked into Brant's potent gray eyes and her heart beat a hundred times per minute. The splash of rain hit the roof above them and poured down the panes as if someone was throwing buckets at the glass. Rain had dampened his hair and gave the impression of a man, or perhaps a bear, awakening from slumber. Except he wasn't awakening. She could see he was as sharp and aware of her presence as she was of his. His shoulders were taut, his entire body perched for some reaction from her.

She shivered from the cold. Her pulse throbbed in her throat.

What would happen between them?

She waited…and waited.

Roughly, he swung back to the fire, away from her. "The rain's so cold, I'm surprised it's not snowing. Get out of those wet boots. Your skirt's soaked along the hem, too." His voice echoed gruffly against the rafters.

He prodded the fire till it burst into higher flames.

"Don't want you to get sick. Take them off and stand by the fire. We'll need them dry by morning."

Cradling her arms for warmth, she looked down at her splotched skirt. He was right.

She lifted her bag, took it to the far corner where the warmth of the fire could still reach her, and rummaged through her dry clothes. She removed her boots and then, making sure he wasn't looking, slid out of her wet skirt and replaced it with another. Unfortunately, she only had one petticoat with her, and it had to be removed to dry.

Water hadn't penetrated her blouse, but her hair was damp.

She took her wet things to the fire and slung them over the back of a chair. Splintering heat from the orange flames seeped into her arms, but she still shivered in her stocking feet.

"Stay near the fire till you're completely warm." He stared at the burning logs. A muscle flicked along his cheek. Rain drizzled down his temples and swirled along the angles of his face.

"What about you?" She held her hands up to the fire. "Your pants are wet, too. And your boots."

He swung around, bold and sure of himself. His gaze trailed down her face and settled on her blouse.

He growled then, a low hum at the back of his throat, just like the grizzly he appeared to be.

In a daring move, he reached up and pulled her down to his lap. She gasped at his speed.

Their lips touched softly. With another yank, he kissed her hard, swooped her off her feet and onto the soft rugs by the fire.

Laid out on her back beneath his body, she felt her pulses come alive with a powerful beat. Her stomach quaked. How could she want a man this much? Someone she shouldn't get involved with. Someone who'd been dead wrong for her sister, and was certain to hurt her, too.

But his lips didn't feel like hurt.

They felt like the rain outside. Pounding at first, then when she grew accustomed to their force, they left her skin raw and burning. He kissed her jaw, her temple, her earlobe, and then nuzzled his face against her throat, kissing and sucking the base of her neck with such heated strokes it sent her heart soaring.

Gasping at his touch, at the huge rise of pleasure in her own body, the ache of wanting Brant, she was surprised when his mouth came back toward hers and he gently touched her lips with his tongue. She opened slightly and his tongue slipped inside, moist and heated and meeting her own in a light swirl.

"Umm…" She'd never truly been kissed as thoroughly as Brant was kissing her now. She never knew this sort of bliss could exist, this fervor between a man and woman, a natural instinct to bond.

To make love.

She wasn't sure where to let him lead her, but she was sure of how she felt. She was ready to please him, ready to take what he had to offer, the time they had alone.

How long and hard she had worked these past two years, preparing to leave for Alaska when her parents weren't keen on her going, finding work with two other nurses at the clinic, finding room and board and a method to pay for her meals.

But she'd done it all alone.

Yet here was Brant, telling her not in so many words, but in the way he held her, that he respected her as a woman, respected her as a companion on this trip, and he was willing to show her more.

Earlier, his attentive reaction to the children they'd met showed he had depth and a tender side to his blunt confidence. To his cocky nature and sure-as-hell-you-love-me attitude. The depth and tenderness had surprised her, just as his physical reaction to her now did.

He pulled away from her mouth, and there, entwined as lovers on the floor, he looked down at the buttons on her lace blouse and back up to her face.

"I'm not sure what to do with you," he said hoarsely.

She swallowed. She was sure herself, but afraid to go forward. Afraid of being the one to say it.

"I know what I want to do." He tipped her chin. "But I'm not sure you're ready."

"I'm ready, Brant." She said the words so softly, they were absorbed in the soft fur of the rugs.

"But…you're a virgin. Right?"

She nodded softly. "Yes…but I am ready."

There came that bearish growl again. He bent his wet head over hers, clamped his hands firmly at the center of her blouse and tugged the buttons open.

She moaned out an exclamation of surprise, even though she knew what was coming. She was totally exposed to him, corset and all.

Drops of rain fell from his hair onto her skin. The sheen glistened off her skin, the tops of her breasts, the arms that clung to his shoulders.

He admired the view, his voice raspy as he spoke.

"I've wanted to do this since the moment I laid eyes on you."

He tugged laces.

Seams parted.

Whalebone shifted.

Breasts appeared.

A corner of his mouth rose in approval.

Heated air from the fire drifted over her damp nipples. She was half-naked with a man. What was she doing? She wasn't this type of woman.

What type was she?

The type who responded to Brant. How could she help herself? He was courageous. Sensitive when he wanted to be. Accepting of others. Helpful and unafraid to work hard.

He lowered his head and kissed her again on the mouth, stroking her face and making her feel adored and cherished.

She wrapped her arms up around his neck.

His damp shirt billowed out and grazed her flesh. Cool, wet cloth clung to her breasts. She felt her nipples stiffen and gooseflesh rise on every part of her. He played with her mouth, gently circling, then digging in with a frenzy. Their tongues met, he swirled his and she followed his lead.

Boldly, she reached up to the buttons on his shirt and undid one, then another and another.

He laughed into her mouth, eager to get out of his wet clothes, clawing out from the icy rain and the heaviness of saturated denim.

She rolled him over toward the fire, and they stopped for a minute when she was poised above him. Her loose brown hair swung over his bare chest and she laughed softly at the teasing expression on his face.

His eyes were the color of deep varnished stone. Without his shirt, the sleek muscles of his chest rippled in the firelight. Drops of dew kissed his skin.

He reached out and cupped her breast. It spilled into his large callused hand. She loved the feel of him, tugging and caressing her bosom, his thumb grazing her nipple, sending delicious tremors through her body as she witnessed the splendor in his eyes.

He watched her breasts for a moment, his gentle stroke making her blood pound with dizzying heat, making her come alive in feminine places, making her throb with moistness and readiness.

His voice was like a gentle strum of a guitar. "I love the way you move."

The knot in her stomach tightened with his touch, with his words, with the look in his eyes.

She wanted him like no other man on the planet, and her realization was both frightening and exhilarating.

* * *

The weight of Victoria's silky breast in his hand, combined with the firelight on her skin, and the sensual stir of her lips, aroused Brant in more places than one.

She straddled him from above, half clothed.

She was a vision with her corset slid down off her breasts. It cinched her narrow waist and uplifted the golden spheres with the large pink nipples that filled his palms. His breath snagged in his throat at her beauty, which any man would expect. But the emotions building inside of him came as an utter surprise.

Why did his heart beat so fast he could barely control it? Why did he yearn to give her everything he could? More than the physical.

His spirit soared when she called his name, when she whispered how much she liked it when he touched her, when she moaned in that feminine way that made him want to do this with her all night long.

"Victoria, I have to know. Are you sure you want this? Now? With me?"

"Yes," she whispered, dipping her face against his cheek. "With you."

He could barely restrain himself, he was so engorged. His body urged him, challenged him, to roll her over and take her as quickly as he could.

But he knew it was important to both of them that he take the time to make this right.

"I want this to be good for you," he murmured against her breast.

"It already is."

"It can be so special, Victoria, feel so unbelievably good."

"It already is," she repeated, and made him smile as he pressed his lips against her nipple.

It was hard and ripe and ready for his mouth. He flicked little circles around the edge as he palmed the underside of her gorgeous breasts. They were smooth and golden and perfect, jutting out in the shape of rich pears.

She grew incredibly still and for a moment he wondered if he was pressing too hard with his tongue, or maybe too soft, or maybe not quite in the right way. But she moaned softly and when he stopped to kiss the other breast, he looked up at her face and she gave him such a daring, trembling smile that he knew his touch was fine.

He kissed her other nipple, stroked it lightly with his warm breath and tongue, then began unlacing the rest of her corset, lace by lace, with such excruciating delay that his body throbbed for need of release. He forced himself to go slow, tugging the last of her stays and sliding the whalebone contraption from her back to the floor.

"Ah, such beauty," he whispered.

He kissed the soft flat plane of her abdomen, the wondrous feminine curve of her waist and the almost invisible downy hairs at her rib cage that were silhouetted in the orange glow of the fire.

She smelled good. Clean, rain-kissed skin, feminine flesh to be licked and stroked and inhaled. She shuddered when he tongued the sensitive area around her belly button and he delighted in her reaction.

He tugged at the waistband of her skirt. "Does this come off?"

"No," she laughed softly. "It's permanently stitched to my body."

"Well, then, we'll have to work around that." But with an expert hand, he undid the button at her side and tugged her fabrics lower, leaving it draped on her hips.

"Hmm." Her lips pressed together with a gentle ribbing. "Not a novice, I see."

"You wouldn't have wanted me as a novice, believe me."

"Why not?"

"I would've been finished already, and snoring at your feet."

"It doesn't take you long?"

He inhaled deeply with an utter sense of peace and happiness, knowing what was about to happen between them. "You drive me to the brink, Victoria, with just one look at those incredibly beautiful breasts."

She smiled shyly, almost embarrassed at his forthright compliment, but he knew she was pleased.

She lowered her body onto his, her warm breasts pressing against him, and kissed him deeply.

Such splendor, being wrapped up in a woman's arms—this woman's arms—as she kissed him thoroughly and passionately, sliding the length of her naked torso against his as if it was the most natural thing in the world.

It was the most natural thing in the world. This union, the coupling between a man and woman in a mutual gesture of loving and respect.

But now she really was driving him insane. How rock-hard he was growing. It was almost painful to resist her. With a playful growl, he rolled her over onto the carpets till she was lying on her back.

"Now what are you going to do?" he teased. "You're trapped."

"Please let me go," she teased in response, pretending she was pleading. "I really do have to go milk the cows, sir. My mama will kill me if I'm late with my chores."

He laughed at her silliness and she giggled as he nibbled the sweet side of her neck.

As she wrapped her arms up around his neck, he swept his hand along her naked side—her underarm, the curve of her rib cage, the pinch of her waist and the swell of her hip. When his roving fingers snagged on her half-slung skirt, he rolled over to release it. He tugged gently then she took over, yanking it off her hips and exposing pantaloons.

He yanked on the billowing cotton. "Off, please."

As she complied, he undid the buttons of his fly and slid out of his pant legs, then drawers, till he was completely naked. She removed her stockings. Perched upright, totally naked as well, she lowered herself slowly down beside him as he stroked the seductive curves of her back. He noted her gaze swept over him, starting at his feet, his thighs, then his manhood.

She said nothing but her throat moved up and down as she swallowed.

"Hmm," she murmured, as both awe and confusion raced through her tone.

"I won't do anything you don't want me to," he told her, hoping to ease her mind, if she was concerned about the fit between them.

"I hope I'm able…to do the right thing. I'm not sure how…"

He smiled at her loveliness. "You'll know how. Instinct will take over."

When she was fully laid back alongside him, he

savored the lushness of her body. Heaven almighty, she was a goddess. Because she was lying on her side, her top breast spilled over at a beautiful angle to the lower one, areolas swollen and pointing at him as if to challenge his lips from staying away.

He couldn't. He lowered his head to kiss the one closest, the silky skin beckoning for a male hand.

Not just yet.

She groaned and closed her eyes for a moment of disappointment and he grinned softly, loving to see her so in need of his touch. When those lovely dark lashes flicked open again, he looked lower, over her body, past the smooth stomach and naked hip to her private spot. Dark curls cut a tender triangle over the area he would soon target, and he sighed in deep satisfaction. Lower still, her calves were nicely rounded and her pretty pink toes reached over to warm his.

They touched only at their feet, and he could hardly wait for more. But he needed to protect her.

He stroked her cheek. "Mind if I get something from your medical bag?"

A frown flickered over her face for the second it took for her to understand.

She nodded as he rolled to the far side of the fireplace, unbuckled the latches, and sought the slender packages of condom sheaths he'd seen inside once, when she'd shuffled through it on the coach. They were obviously intended for any of her patients in need of such privacies.

He had no problem sliding one on, as he was fully erect. In fact, he hoped the condom layer would help slow down his reaction to her.

When he turned around and spotted her again in all her glory, he knew that would be impossible.

Her glossy brown hair trailed down the soft angles of her shoulders and splayed across her dangling breasts. The indent of her waist, the length of her thighs, and that sweet dark triangle made his mouth water and his erection harden.

She gazed at him with such lust in her eyes, his beautiful Victoria, that his throat tightened with emotion. He moved toward her, intent on making her shout his name.

Chapter Twelve

Dazzled by Brant's physique as she lay on her back, Victoria rose on her elbows and watched him. He approached from her feet and splayed his knees on either side of her legs. He ran his hot hand up her calf, over her knee and up along her thigh. Every stroke was bliss on her skin, giving rise to gooseflesh, and feathery tickles in her stomach, and a clamping and releasing of her breath.

Then he lay down behind her on the plush cotton rug, spooning her and pushing one hand underneath her so that it came up to nestle her breast. He slid his other large hand in between her legs, letting it rest on her inner thigh. Such an intimate way to hold her.

"It'll be better for you like this," he whispered

in between tiny kisses on her upper arm. "The first time."

"How do you mean?"

"It'll help you—" He stopped suddenly, as if changing his mind about explaining it to her. "You'll see."

She lifted her arm up and over his head, exposing her breast. He took the opportunity to lower his mouth to her rib cage. The soft kisses and the stirring of his tongue felt like flower petals on her flesh.

She leaned back against him, wanting to feel the full length of his nakedness.

He complied readily, pressing his front flush with her behind. His erection was firm and solid and so very large, sliding against her buttocks. She groaned with the possibilities running through her imagination. Would he enter her from behind? Was that possible? She'd only ever imagined it, in her private fantasies, from the front.

She started wiggling against him and he moaned. "Not yet."

He backed away an inch or so, much to her frustration, and slid his hand farther between her thighs. With daring confidence, he inched closer and closer toward her center, setting every nerve of her skin on fire from his touch, making her hold her breath with anticipation.

He found her.

His fingers were gentle and he gave no indication of surprise or embarrassment to be doing this with her, to be so bold in his moves and expectations.

It was a newfound experience for her, to be naked with Brant and so fully exposed, physically and emotionally. She worried about the pain this night might cause, and whether she'd be pleasurable for him, or good enough, and live up to what he thought the night should be.

His fingers moved in the slickness he found.

"Victoria," he hummed in satisfaction.

Sensations she'd never felt with a man before made her senses come alive. His fingers slid between her folds, back and forth, creating tension and a marvelous pulsation. She moved her hips back and forth along his hand, understanding now what he'd meant by it being better this way the first time. He was so intent on ensuring pleasure for her that she must thank him later....

"So nice," she whispered to the night air, the sounds of her voice getting lost in the crackle of the fire.

He rubbed deeper and firmer and she was so moist now his hand was sliding between her legs. When he inserted a finger inside, she was so startled she tensed. But then the feeling of his fingers all wrapped up down there, hitting all the right places, excited her to a feverish pitch.

He rocked harder and rubbed faster until she was no longer sure what his fingers were doing, only how utterly great they felt. With his other hand beneath her breast, he reached up and tweaked her nipple, and she was a goner.

The rippling sensations shot like a bullet through her, to a peak that made her muscles clench and release, quivering beneath his expert hand, exploding the tension to an exhilarating thunder. He was right. Her movements came instinctively and she rocked against him.

When the last shudder softened to a whisper, he removed his hand, kissed her shoulder and nuzzled against her ear.

"I'll give you an A plus," she whispered.

He smiled softly. "I'll take it."

She lay there, lazy and heavy, in the luxury of the fire. Was she in heaven?

"You best get moving, miss. You've got cows to milk."

She smiled. "You're a funny man."

"Am I?"

He rolled her over, suddenly much more serious, then rose to his knees and towered over her, his erection poised and ready. His gaze seared her somewhere deep inside. A permanent scorch on her soul.

Totally uninhibited, surprising herself, she looked up and admired his body—the muscles that balled at his shoulders, the broad chest, hard abdomen and his huge shaft.

He waited so patiently for her.

She splayed her legs and allowed him closer. Gently, he pressed forward, rubbing her hot opening with the tip of his shaft. Could he fit? she wondered.

Her muscles were relaxed from her orgasm, and perhaps this would make it smoother and easier.

He stroked her softly, her thigh, her belly, and reached up and cupped a breast as he thrust deeper.

Then the pain came. Sheer pain that threatened to tear her apart. She must have stiffened, for he stopped, frowned and gently eased her lifted thigh back to a relaxed position.

"Almost there," he murmured.

She trusted Brant. Believed that he would do right by her. And when that final thrust came and he broke through, the pain was shattering. She took a moment to breathe.

He waited. Small drops of sweat glistened off his forehead as he waited to see if she was all right.

Yes, she'd be fine. She slid her bottom lower against his, silently indicating he continue.

And so he did.

Her dear and beloved Brant. He thrust himself into her, and she marveled at the intensity of the moment, the stretch of her muscles, the diminishing of the pain till she felt nothing but the deep saturation of being with Brant in the most intimate coupling imaginable.

And when it was time for his release and his climax shuddered through him, she watched the ardent expression on his handsome face, the glaze of sheen on his perfect body, the glistening of his dark eyes as he looked deep into hers.

"Victoria," he murmured. "Victoria…Victoria…"

Many hours later, heavy with sleep, Victoria slipped into a dream….

"Victoria!" her mother called up the stairs. "Victoria! Fix your hair! Company's here! Brant is here for Sarah!"

Thirteen years old and bursting with eagerness to learn all she could about the birds and the bees, Victoria rushed out of her bedroom in her calico housedress and stood at the top of the stairs as Sarah answered the door. Brant swung in, lean and muscled in his early twenties. He'd been riding today, for instead of trousers and topcoat, he wore a leather vest and those denim jeans her mother so despised. Miner's pants, her ma called them when he wasn't around. *Sarah, why must your beau wear those miner's pants?*

Victoria played with her long braid as she watched her sister with Brant.

Were they going to kiss?

She watched but it didn't happen.

However, Sarah slipped her hand beneath his arm to lead him to the dining room. Finally, a physical connection. Victoria wondered how it would feel to touch a boy. She watched them go, disappointed she'd be getting no more lessons, for the moment, on the proper behavior when a suitor came calling....

A crack of thunder woke her with a start.

Brant, in a deep sleep beside her, beneath the covers in the bedroom with their private fireplace softly burning, reached out and stroked her arm. Here in Alaska, many years after her adolescent fantasies, it was Brant who'd taught her about the birds and the bees, after all.

"Just the storm. Don't worry. Go back to sleep."

He looped a strong arm over her waist and nestled in behind her, both of them still naked. It was freeing to be with him.

How would it feel in the light of morning?

Still freeing? Would he still want her? For how long?

Forever?

Part of her was still that romantic thirteen-year-old girl who was eager to know about the details and possibilities of a life filled with sex and love.

The other part was a grown woman. A woman who had seen trouble in her life. Had been told she wasn't good enough to marry a preacher. And was now lying with her sister's former beau.

She didn't feel guilty about the last bit. Sarah had forgotten about Brant, otherwise how could she have married Martin?

Brant was no longer Sarah's.

But was he Victoria's?

She hoped and trembled for the possibility.

Later that morning, Walker Dixon rubbed the coarse bristles along his chin, chomped down on his chewing tobacco, and spit a gob of juicy liquid into the alcove of the cabin beyond his father's bed. Two other men stood nearby, watching. Gutter, and a railroad engineer who knew a little about broken bones, the townsfolk had said, which was why Dixon had called for him.

Dixon looked at his sleeping father and winced. "Christ almighty, it's come to this, has it?"

His pa was in a deep sleep. The old man, wearing long johns stained with soup and coffee and various other foods they'd tried feeding him, still cut a fine figure of a man. Over six feet tall, he still had a full head of white hair and muscles on his frame, although lots of his peers had none. But gone was his color.

Gutter had shaved him this morning, and his face clearly reflected how much weight he'd lost in the past two weeks.

They'd ripped off his left sleeve so that his broken upper arm could be visible for cleaning and bandaging.

But dammit, it hadn't helped much. The bandage was stained with yellow pus as the engineer had unwrapped it to have a closer look.

Dixon squinted at the engineer, who'd brought a sack of tools. "Gangrene, you say?"

The man beneath the black sombrero trembled. "'Fraid so."

Dixon swallowed hard past the lump of despair in his throat. Blast them all to hell. Every last one of the doctors and nurses in Skagway who weren't here to help his old man.

They were supposed to be here two damn weeks ago.

Dixon's heart skittered as he watched his father's Adam's apple snag along his throat with his uneasy breathing. It was torture looking at him. This was the same jovial man who'd spent hours and days and months teaching a young Dixon how to shoot a coin off a man's shoulder. How to skin a deer. How to rob a bank and how to aim for a man's heart.

His pa had taught him that the world didn't provide nothin' for no one, and it was up to Dixon to get what he wanted when he wanted it.

Son of a bitch. And now here was Dixon having to make the most horrific of choices for dear old Pa.

Dixon took a deep breath. Rolled the wad of tobacco to the other side of his mouth and tongued the pit of liquid.

"Chop it off."

Gutter and the railroad man gasped at the order, even though they likely guessed it was coming.

The railroad man set his tools to the floor and started pulling out his various supply of saws. The man wasn't even an engineer anymore. He'd come to Alaska like everyone else, searching for gold and a future.

"When you're done," Dixon added, "make sure you burn it."

"Yes, sir."

Dixon didn't want the contamination overtaking the cabin. The cool air inside the alcove sliced raw down his throat. Sentiment stung the back of his eyes. Then a deep churning resentment throbbed inside his chest, and a need to taste revenge.

"Gutter, give the orders. When the doctor or nurse arrives at the pass, tell the men to welcome them. Then bring 'em straight to me. They're gonna burn in hell for what they've done."

"Yes, sir." Respectfully, Gutter tugged his hat back onto his dark head of hair. He swung away, but just at that moment, Dixon's pa grumbled something.

The engineer leaned closer to listen, maybe forgetting he was holding the clean blade he'd picked out. Then much to Dixon's surprise and glee, his dear old pa still had enough wits about him to pick up the gun lying at his side. He blasted the engineer straight through the chest.

The man hit the floor in a heap of blood, instantly dead.

"No one's takin' my arm just yet," said Pa.

Dixon's heart pounded with pride and pleasure at seeing the old man's strength return. "Christ, Pa. Still got good aim."

Brant tucked his clothes inside his duffel bag and watched Victoria pack hers on the other side of the bed.

His eyes burned with the need for more sleep, since they'd only gotten about two hours, but his limbs were warm and heavy with the aftermath of their sensuous night. It had been spectacular to bed Victoria.

But guilt gnawed at him as he watched the soft

turn of her cheek against the glowing embers of the fire, and the way her dark hair fell against her blouse. It pleased him to watch the way her waist twisted as she bent and turned, and the way her breasts strained beneath the layers of cotton fabrics.

His heart kicked up speed, knowing he'd felt the warmth of her breasts last night and had placed his hands where no man had before.

It was an honor, and he wanted more. That much he knew. What he didn't know was how to get there with her. Or if he could.

How she'd feel if he disclosed he was after Walker Dixon; that he'd been after him for two years. That for more than the past week as he'd traveled knee to knee with her, he'd been keeping bits of the truth to himself.

Did she deserve to know?

Yes.

Could he tell her?

Maybe.

He'd risk losing this, though. The trust in her gaze as she swung up from packing the last of her things and smiled shyly at him, as though they were newlyweds on their honeymoon.

God, he felt sick inside.

All right, he told himself. He would tell her and tell her soon.

"Victoria," he began.

She patted her carpetbag and came to stand behind him. She wrapped those loving arms around him and nuzzled up tight. The sweet, soft pillow of her cheek warmed his shoulder blade.

"What is it, Brant?"

He opened his mouth to tell her, but was interrupted by a loud knock at the door.

Her face jarred off his shoulder.

He grabbed her hands at his waist. "Ignore it."

She laughed softly. "How can we do that? These people put us up for the night."

"Just stay here with me." He yanked her around, looping his arms around her so that they stood face-to-face.

"I'd love to, but we've got to get moving. The weather's cleared. The sun's out and somewhere out there, Cooper's waiting for us."

"I understand that, but just for a moment longer."

The knock came again, only louder. Zachary called, "You folks in there? Your horse is getting restless. And Alberta's got breakfast going."

"Breakfast," Victoria said to Brant. "How can we refuse that?"

He tried to grab her as she slipped away, but she scooted out of his clutch, as though they were playing a game of tag. But he was stone-cold serious.

He'd never before wanted to share this much with anyone. He'd always been the type of man who kept to himself. Did as he pleased. Thought of life in terms of short-range goals rather than long ones. Last night, Victoria had brought something out of him that he'd never seen coming. A desire to think about his life and who he might want to be spending it with two years from now. Or three. Or five. Or ten.

"Coming!" Victoria bounced to the door with the same energy and enthusiasm he recalled when he'd first met her and the rest of the Windhaven family.

And that, of course, brought on another rush of guilt.

Chapter Thirteen

Within an hour, Brant and Victoria had eaten breakfast, said goodbye to the Ford family, and were again galloping through the woods, alone. This time, as Victoria sat perched on the horse in front of him, Brant had the luxury of brushing against her warm cheek on occasion, kissing her neck and letting her know she was constantly on his mind.

That was part of the problem.

He couldn't stop thinking about her.

The memory of the night and all they'd done with each other aroused him all over again, when he should be concentrating on riding.

The rain had washed out all potential tracks of the men they were following. Fortunately, it was still very early morning and they were making good time.

The sun had barely risen over the mountains, but the sky was clear and bright and would soon dry most of the mud from last night.

Cooper and the two men who'd taken him couldn't possibly have ridden straight through the storm. And since they'd skipped a night of sleep the night before, Brant was hoping they might be dawdling this morning, taking an extra few hours, and generally being overconfident they were miles ahead of Brant and Victoria.

If they even believed that they were being chased.

Brant hoped not, for that meant more mistakes due to arrogance.

Victoria, thankfully, was well aware of the need to focus on riding today.

She said very little as they broke for lunch, rode a couple of hours, rested the horse, then rode again till dinner. They were making extraordinary time, but Brant was careful not to get overeager himself, in case the mare strained a muscle or carelessly slipped on the slope of a mountain.

When it was nightfall and the horse began to breathe more heavily, Brant stopped in a sheltered corner of the woods.

"We're getting close to the mountain pass," he told her. "A couple more hours of riding at most."

"That's where Dixon's men will be?"

"Yeah."

"You think we should approach in broad day-light, don't you?"

He nodded. "And the horse needs to rest. We'll stop here for the night."

"Whatever's best, Brant. You're the expert in riding and tracking."

That was the other part of the problem. He wasn't owning up to just how much his time was still devoted to tracking outlaws in the middle of nowhere.

Without being a bragging sort of man, he confessed there were very few men who could outride or outdistance him in one day.

When he'd first started, he'd been a weak rider. Mediocre shooter. Didn't know one berry from the next in terms of survival, and hadn't been able to build a fire unless he had a match.

Those days were gone and he was proud of what he'd accomplished.

He bristled at the thought that he'd have to give it up for anyone.

Is that what life with a woman would be like? Giving up the things he loved most and was good at?

And what about the folks who needed him to bring criminals to justice? Mothers who'd lost their sons to cutthroats. Fathers who'd seen their daughters raped. Folks who'd spent decades scraping and saving their money in a bank, only to see a roving gang put a trigger to the teller's head and snatch it all away.

Life wasn't fair, but he was here to make it a little bit fairer.

Most of the men he sought were brutal killers, running from one state to the next and making it nearly impossible for lawmen to follow. Brant didn't mind following. And if not him, who then would go?

It satisfied him to know how many men he'd put behind bars in the past five years. Twenty-seven of the roughest, cruelest men that ever roamed the planet.

Walker Dixon would be the twenty-eighth.

Did Brant have to give it up for Victoria?

Hell, he thought as they unpacked in solitude, she wasn't even asking him that.

She wasn't asking anything of him.

He watched her lay out her bedroll at the foot of the small fire, humming softly as she worked, content to help him collect kindling, water the horse by the river, prepare something to eat.

She was an amazing woman.

He just wasn't sure what he could give her or

promise her, or even what she wanted from this time together.

And until he figured out what he wanted, maybe it was best to keep his thoughts to himself.

And keep his distance from Victoria. Making love to her again would have to wait until they cleared things between them and rescued Cooper.

Even though she wasn't voicing a hope for a future with Brant, it was being said loud and clear in her actions. She smiled at him over the fire, brushed her hair in that feminine way, and patted down his bedroll to make sure it was nice and smooth for his liking.

Dammit, her unspoken words of expectation roared through the silence.

Victoria tried not to worry, but it had been half an hour since they'd gone to bed, and Brant still hadn't come near her. Her thighs shuddered from the strain of riding all day, her back ached, and her bottom was sore from a combination of riding and spending the evening before with Brant.

But she still desired him.

He'd checked the riverbank and woods for signs of intruders; he'd listened to the calls of the owls and wolves. They were completely alone and safe.

"Brant?" she whispered, gazing into the fire. They were both facing it to keep warm. And that was another thing. Why not sleep together? He had insisted they would be warmer this way, if they both faced the fire and one didn't have to sleep behind the other.

"Hmm?"

"Did I do something wrong?"

"No, darlin', no."

She let the silence sit.

He broke it first. "It's just that…I don't think it's fair to you if I come inching over."

"But I like when you inch over."

"And I like inching over," he assured her.

"But?"

He sighed. "If I inch over, I don't plan on inching back."

"That sounds exciting."

"It's not fair to you—"

"Not fair to come here and kiss me?"

He let out a sigh of amusement.

"Don't you want to kiss me, Brant?"

"Victoria."

"Well, don't you? I liked it so much last night."

"Ahh," he groaned. "How am I supposed to fight you?"

"Why are you trying to fight me?"

"I'm trying to fall asleep."

"Come here and rest on my shoulder, then."

She looked over at him, straining her neck to get

her fill of Brant. She gazed on the lips that looked so firm at a distance but were so gentle when they made their way up her body. The strong arms, the sensual fingertips, the long legs that stretched forever before reaching the end of his blanket.

With a glint of mischief, she lifted her covers when his eyelids opened and he looked over at her. She exposed the undone buttons of her blouse and revealed the swell of her breasts. She'd removed her corset for sleeping simply because it was so uncomfortable, but she'd retained her chemise and blouse, in case of emergency.

His gaze lowered to her breasts and a lazy smile drifted over his face. "You're trying to entice me."

"Is it working?"

His soft groan was almost drowned in the crackle of burning logs. Then he jumped to his feet and dove under her covers.

"Yup."

When his arms wrapped around her and his thighs pressed against hers, his reservations seem to melt. The two of them were together again, and he did want her.

Her instincts took over when he kissed her neck, his lips inching up in a pace that was torturously slow, but deliciously heated.

He found the hem of her blouse and yanked it out of the waistband of her skirt. His large hand shimmied up and over her chemise, cupping the round swells of her breasts, and he marveled at the way her nipples bulged and protruded through the cloth. He bit the side of her mouth playfully, ran his tongue along her jaw, and when his heated mouth reached the hollow of her throat, she gave herself to Brant.

Brant kissed her again, savoring their time together in the bedroll, vowing he'd go slow with her and please her till she'd always come to him like this.

His senses drummed within him, his heart thundering like water over the wheel of a gristmill. He inhaled the scent of her skin, loved the taste of her flesh beneath his lips, and couldn't get enough of looking at her heavenly body, trapped by the fire's glow as he slipped off her chemise.

Golden light cocooned her breasts; it emphasized their jiggling and hypnotic bounce, and the pink virginal tone of her nipples.

Could this all be for him? On whose tally did he deserve a woman so beautiful and giving?

"Are you sore from last night?"

"A bit."

"We'll go slow."

"Maybe we should go faster, so I get more practice."

Her sense of humor amused him. He tugged at

her skirt, then the clothes beneath until she was totally bare.

His mouth watered as though looking at a splendid banquet of food, as though he hadn't eaten in months. He savored the rise and fall of her rib cage lifting those remarkable breasts, the indentation of her tight stomach, the smooth thighs, the shock of dark curls, the feminine toes.

"Victoria, I'll never get enough of you."

A quirk of sentiment lifted the soft corners of her mouth. "That's what I like to hear, Brant."

She yanked on his buttons, tore open his shirt, ran those lovely slender fingers up and down the muscles of his chest, and yanked the sleeves off his arms. She spared no haste in undoing his fly, and he basked in the sensation of being disrobed by Victoria.

"You learn fast," he teased.

"I was always good in school."

In a great sigh of pleasure, she slid backward for a moment to study her handiwork when she'd removed all his clothes. "And what a fine man you are."

He reached up and stroked her cheek, this wondrous beauty who seized his gaze and stared back at him with all the heaving emotion he was feeling, too. With a single fingertip, he trailed down the center of her breastbone, soft and dewy beneath his touch, her skin shimmering with health, an erotic display of sensuality.

He grew harder with every second, throbbing in places that came alive only when she was near.

"You smell like the wind," he said, burying his face in her hair. "And the sun and the moon."

"Brant, you do know how to please me."

She caressed the inside of his waist and he kissed her collarbone and the sweet skin of her shoulder. She shuddered at his touch, while the muscles in his gut contracted. His body knew what was coming and he couldn't stop himself from reacting. Every stroke of her fingers ignited every cell he had, from the hairs at the back of his neck to the flesh that arose on his arms, to the exquisite, silent torture of his erection.

In a graceful swoop, he reached for her medicine bag and took out the sheath he needed.

She watched, completely still, waiting for him to get it on, smiling gently in shyness.

When he was ready, he bent on his knees before her, planted a palm on each of her kneecaps and gently nudged her open. She arched her back and looked at him with such wild abandon, he could take the torture no more.

With a passion and excitement he could barely contain, he leaned forward and slid himself along the ivy of her curls, against the moistness, then deeper to penetrate the folds.

She gasped and wrapped her legs around his waist. His heart leaped when they connected. She blazed a trail of fire along his back before her fingers dug into the cords of his muscles, her breasts heaving beneath him, her soft moans so feminine and enticing.

When he was totally wet from her, and she was squirming her bottom as if unable to restrain herself, she panted, "Now, Brant. Give it to me now."

"Just a touch."

"The whole thing."

"Let's take our time."

She let out a frustrated reply. Then she simply nudged her bottom forward and that was all he could take. He couldn't fight her, couldn't resist her, even though he was trying with everything he had.

He slid into her heat, closed his eyes momentarily at how wholly she engulfed him, how natural and exciting and feverish their bond.

She squeezed her eyes closed.

"Does it hurt?" he asked gently, concern making him stop.

"No. It's just…you fill me up completely."

Aye, and wasn't that the truth?

"You fill me up, too, Victoria. You take over my mind and body and soul."

She gave another moan of contentment. He felt her relax beneath him, and he slowly started the rhythm that would bring them both to the brink.

He thumbed her from the top, sliding his fingers against the slick button, hoping to please her and show her how he felt, not daring to stop and think of tomorrow.

She seemed to unfold like the fresh petals of a rose in sunshine. Victoria, who'd never been touched, blossomed and undulated against him, caught in the feeling of his fingertips pressed against her, the man inside of her, the magical spell of the moment.

Crisp Alaskan air surrounded them, but the blazing fire kept them warm. He barely noticed the heat on his skin, the nip of the wind behind him, and the chirping of night birds on the overhead branches.

He watched her beneath him as her muscles came to climax, her golden skin against the fire, the shifting mounds of her breasts tipped with pink nipples, her lips ripe with the sound of his name, the earth-pounding pulse of her muscles squeezing his shaft as if begging for every drop he had.

She came first and he adored the way she arched, the way she gave herself to him completely, unabashed to display her nude figure and expose the way her body strained with her climax. It was an image he would never forget.

And a feeling he wished he could capture forever. The release of his own climax as she was finishing with hers, the complete fulfillment of this sensual act, the pinnacle of sensations.

When he was finished, he opened his eyes to the beauty who lay beneath him. Her hair was a flowing river, cascading over her breasts and silhouetting the curves of her cheeks and lips.

For some reason, she found their position, or perhaps their abandonment to the moment, humorous. She breathed out a soft laugh and he followed. They did get carried away together, didn't they?

He bent over, laughed into the side of her neck and withdrew.

He didn't know why, but there was a lot of laughter around her, and touching and kissing and sentiments he hadn't felt in such a very long time.

Many hours later, after they were fully clothed and he had tucked his arms around her, he sought solace in his sleep. There was lots of laughter now, since they'd become intimate, but he knew there was a serious side to things of which Victoria was unaware.

If they had any hopes of keeping this up between them, this newfound discovery of feelings for each other, he had to come clean.

She had to know he was still a bounty hunter and that he hadn't left that part of his life behind.

Adjusting his shoulder against the firm ground, he found himself trying to sleep against a flat rock. It dug into him, no matter how he tried to find a softer spot. Maybe it was a symbol of the difficult spot he found himself in with Victoria.

He'd decided not to tell her during the night, for they both needed their rest. And didn't things always weigh heavier on the mind in the darkness? The worry and fret that came with unsolved problems. Things always looked better in the light of day.

Tomorrow, he told himself. But when his eyes opened again as dawn was breaking and Victoria was nudging him, he jolted awake with a fear that wouldn't leave him.

The time had come to tell her and he wasn't sure how she'd take it.

"Wake up, sleepyhead," she murmured against his temple, kissing his unshaven jaw and melting those sensuous curves against him. "Wake up, Brant."

Chapter Fourteen

Victoria enjoyed the way her cheek fit against Brant's shoulder. The sun was barely up, breaking through the fog and the mountains, but she was eager to leave to follow after Cooper and knew Brant would be, too.

He rustled beneath her, opened his eyes and took a look around the campfire.

"The fog's awful thick," he replied to her nudges. "We've got a bit of time before we ride out, so let's…get ready and go over our plans."

Plans? So he was feeling it, too? The possibility of a future? Or was he referring to plans about chasing after Cooper? Her stomach turned in those funny little swirls of excitement, as it had done for hours last night as Brant had made love to her.

"I'd like that."

With a ready smile and quick kiss to Brant's shoulder, Victoria got up, finished dressing and started on breakfast.

The red embers of the firepit didn't take much to reignite. Then the aroma of pan-fried smoked meat the Finch brothers had given them wafted through the mist around them. She wore her duster to ward off the early September chill, and thought about the night with Brant as she watched him put on his holster and pack up their things.

What a night it was. He was much more tender and caring than she'd ever considered. She chastised herself for thinking, for the past five years, that he was so much less of a man than he actually was.

He was thoughtful and considerate. Skilled at what he did, whether it was tending to his horse or holding a gun up to a menacing stranger.

And he was a very passionate lover.

The memory of him caressing her face, holding her naked body and kissing every inch of it, made her optimistic of what he might say to her this morning.

But she wasn't a starry-eyed adolescent.

She understood that relationships between men and women could be complicated. Lord only knew, as she'd offered her nursing skills to various people she'd met, she'd seen her share of marriages here in Alaska.

Some were prearranged by parents, two or three were mail-order brides, some had sprung quickly from onboard the ships that carried them here. But it didn't seem to matter how they'd started, though. Some of the marriages were solid. Some seemed strained. And some ended bitterly in separation.

Living in Alaska was hard.

Seemed everything a person did had to be done from scratch, since there were no towns that'd been here before the gold rush. Supplies were limited. Support from family in the lower states was practically nonexistent, save for the occasional letter.

But she'd found Brant.

Or rather, rediscovered him, as she liked to think of it.

And it wasn't that she was thinking he might propose to her. It was that they'd shared two incredible nights together, and she wanted more.

She thought he did, too.

And just where were they headed? That's perhaps what he wanted to discuss.

After tending to the horse, Brant made his way toward her. She enjoyed watching the way he walked. That long, confident stride that reflected pride in who he was. Why had that walk ever irritated her?

With a cheerful whirl, she set the skillet on a large boulder beside her.

"Breakfast is ready."

He ran his long fingers through his thick dark hair and came to join her.

"Brant, I'm sorry."

"For what?"

"That I misjudged you all these years. I thought you were out only for yourself. That people you loved, or appeared to love, came second in your life. Maybe even that you were cold and arrogant."

"Whoa," he said. "That's a lot to swallow."

He said it with a bit of a smile, but she sensed by the tension in his face that he was carefully mulling her words.

"Look how far you've come. You have a steady occupation. A bodyguard and a trail guide. Those are two respectable jobs. Maybe not the politics your father wanted, but you made something of yourself."

His eyelashes flicked. He twisted his lips in concentration. His bristly cheeks fell into a flat expression.

She handed him a plate, ever conscious of the time. She wanted to sit here for hours with him, but they had to be ready to leave soon, to follow Cooper's trail.

He took the plate, the biscuits and the cut of meat, but though she bit into hers, he just stared at his.

Her duster was parted, revealing her skirts. He placed his hand on her knee, and the warmth seeped through the fabric into her skin. It felt right, sitting here with him.

"Aren't you going to eat?"

He removed the pleasant weight of his hand from her knee. A cold spot remained. And she felt suddenly affected by the chill and the fog.

He picked up the biscuit and bit into it. The silence and his mood permeated through the mist.

Something was wrong.

After a lull, he set down his plate on a boulder. "I've got a confession to make."

Her stomach tightened with the words. She didn't like this. Not one bit. She finished with her plate and set it down on her lap.

She waited.

Restless, he jumped to his feet and kicked at the fire to smother it. The sound of dirt hitting flames seared through the cool air. She shivered at the clumsy sound.

"What is it?" she asked.

He swallowed and shoved his hands into the pockets of his suede jacket, looking down at the broken fire. He was still without his hat, and as the morning sun bit through an opening in the fog behind him, it bounced off his hair and silhouetted the broad shoulders, the square stance, the long legs encased in denim.

However, the rugged curves and crags of his face remained in shadow and she couldn't quite read him.

"You already know some about Walker Dixon."

"Yeah. So this is about that criminal?" She exhaled long and deep, her shoulders lowering in relief. "For a minute there, I thought it was about you and me."

He paced the pounded dirt. "It is about you and me."

His words were gently spoken, with a hint of pain almost, and that was when she knew something awful was coming.

Her heart took a leap forward and hammered against her ribs. Her eyes widened and her nostrils flared, waiting for…for something.

"Walker Dixon is wanted in twelve states and territories."

"Right."

"He's done some terrible things."

"So you said."

"And now his men have taken Cooper."

"You're not trying to tell me you think they've already dragged Cooper—"

"No, not yet. They need him in Glitter Mountain first."

"We have to hurry, then."

"We do. But what I'm saying is I've been after Walker Dixon for two years already."

She didn't quite understand. "Two?"

He stopped pacing six feet away and turned around to face her—the striking frame of a man standing tall between the trunks of bare trees.

"I'm still a bounty hunter, Victoria."

Her plate slid off her skirt. He rushed to catch it and she rose to her feet in alarm. He caught the plate and set it down beside her as she walked to the edge of the fire.

She crossed her arms. They jittered from the chill, or maybe from the anxiety welling up inside of her.

"Let me get this straight. You are still a bounty hunter."

"Yeah."

"And what you're saying is…you've been after Walker Dixon this whole time."

"Yeah."

"You knew…when we left Skagway…" Her voice trailed off. "That's why you took this job. You didn't take it as a bodyguard. You took it because it would bring you closer to him."

He nodded, his forehead lowered, studying the expressions moving across her face.

"How am I supposed to feel, Brant?"

"I was hoping you'd understand. This is my job."

"You weren't hoping that. You kept this from me because you knew it would upset me. Otherwise, it wouldn't be so hard to tell me."

His shoulders heaved. His dark eyes sparked. "Hell, I've got to be honest. This is more than a job to me. This is how I contribute to the world."

She clenched her jaw.

"If it were you out there, if Dixon had burned down your family home, with your folks still in it, wouldn't you want someone to catch the guilty man?"

She winced.

"Well, that person is me. I'm volunteering."

A hollow feeling found its mark in the deep pit of her stomach. "Why don't you let the law take care of it?"

"Because it can't. Dixon scurries from state to state to territory and that's how he gets away."

She shook her head. "You're going to leave me," she whispered. "You'll desert me just like you did before. Just like you did Sarah."

He stepped back, shaking his head to vow he wouldn't, but she kept going.

"After Walker Dixon, there'll be someone else

and someone else and someone else.... All the way from here to California, Wyoming to New York."

He shook his head to deny it, and opened his mouth to say something more, but whatever he was thinking went unsaid.

After another heartbeat, he voiced his thoughts. "I'm good at what I do. And someone's got to do it."

She blinked, heartbroken at how the conversation had turned.

"Wait a minute." She scratched her forehead and thought back several days. She moved away and paced by the dying fire. Her skirts whirled about her boots. "Wait just one minute. That day we met, outside Colburne Stables, at the stagecoach. You apprehended those three horse thieves."

He puckered his mouth in a note of apology, maybe knowing what was coming.

"You took so long at the deputy marshal's office because there was a bounty on their heads. You wanted to make sure the deputy marshal got the facts straight and that your name was attached to the reward."

"It's how I earn my living. They were criminals charged with a crime. My priority was getting them to the law."

She looked down at her boots then back at the

man who had so disappointed her. "Then why must you keep it all a secret?"

"I'm not. I'm telling you, aren't I?"

She shook her head, sorrow creeping through her as densely as the fog surrounding them. "I think you've already deserted me, Brant."

He didn't come to her.

He didn't touch her, or hold her, or murmur that her grievances were unfounded. His eyes shimmered with all the unsaid sadness that affected him, too, at what was slipping from their fingers.

And to think that her morning had started off on such a dawn of hope and dreams for spending many more days with Brant.

Brant felt numb inside. Twenty minutes later as they packed the rest of their supplies and prepared to head out, half of him wanted to grab Victoria by the shoulders and tell her how much he wanted to be a part of her life. To stay in Skagway and be the ever-loving man who awoke in her bed every morning and stacked her firewood in the evening.

The other part of him wanted to shout that he could bloody well do what the hell he wanted, when he wanted. That she had no business rifling through his affairs and questioning his strengths as a man, his beliefs in sharing his life with a woman, and even making him question if he wanted a family of his own one day.

For sure as hell, that was what they were talking about here.

She wanted stability and assurances.

He was offering sporadic nights together and no promises of anything secure.

Dammit, what irked him most was that she knew him so well. She knew him from St. Louis and she knew him now.

And hell, he hadn't changed.

But so damn what?

A sudden noise from the faraway thickness of the woods jerked him to the present situation.

She heard it, too, for she froze, standing by the mare. They looked at each other and he brought a finger up to his lips to indicate quiet.

Though the weather had cleared somewhat, it was still foggy. He couldn't see more than ten yards ahead of him, so it was difficult to say what or who was coming.

Could be a wild animal.

The horse nickered. Victoria patted its nose, settling the mare as they continued to listen.

Voices.

Men.

Brant's breath trapped solid in his lungs. Who were they? He strained forward. Two men, very distinctive, echoed above the bare branches of the trees.

And they were headed this way.

His heart kicked into speed, fear for Victoria and fear for himself.

He wasn't sure if the men were friends or foes.

Brant dropped the skillet he was lacing to his saddlebag, right there in the weeds, and motioned to Victoria to back the horse up slowly toward the ravine. They had to get the mare out of view of the trail.

With a frantic rush at the horse and a nod to Brant, Victoria understood instantly what he meant.

Smoothly and silently, she edged the horse backward, soothing the beast.

He scoured the site for anything visible that might give them away. Their bedrolls remained on the ground, as did their saddlebags, but the shrubs covered them from sight so Brant didn't have to worry about retrieving them.

They stood behind the horse and got it behind a clump of scraggly pines, enough for cover.

The voices grew louder, rumbling through the trees, slicing through the fog. "I didn't say keep going. I said slow down."

"Why the hell would you tell me to slow down in a thunderstorm?"

Brant recognized the voices. They were coming

from the two criminals who'd taken Cooper. Mulroy and Thorpe were their names, according to the Ford family.

He looked to Victoria, who nodded in recognition.

Was Cooper with them?

If so, he wasn't talking. And they were still covered by fog.

Brant tensed as he peered around the pine needles, barely noticing the fragrance as he scouted for the young medical student through the hazy mist.

Nothing.

Then around a bend, twenty feet away, a horse appeared, followed by one of the men. Behind him came Cooper, leading his horse, then the third and final man walking behind Cooper.

Cooper slumped along, wincing and limping. The side of his face was dirt-streaked and swollen, as though he'd been beaten up.

Victoria gasped softly beside Brant.

"Is he hurt?" She shuddered and whispered into Brant's shoulder, "What have they done to him?"

Chapter Fifteen

Stricken with fear for Cooper as she hid among the shrubs and trees beside Brant, Victoria watched the three men approach on the dirt path. She longed to reach out to comfort her friend. Her argument with Brant flew out of her mind. Nothing else mattered at this moment except the struggling doctor. With his shoulders slumped, clothes rumpled and his entire left side coated with a layer of dirt, Cooper looked forlorn.

"Don't give up," she whispered.

Brant pressed his shoulder against hers and nudged her gently with his weight. "That's why I wasn't able to see their tracks late yesterday. Not because they were washed out by the rain. But because they were behind us, not in front."

"He fell off his horse," Victoria added. "That's why he's limping."

Brant peered closer. "Yeah, you can see it from the mud on his left side. And his left cheek is swollen."

So they hadn't beaten him, she thought with some relief. He'd fallen. "Maybe that's what slowed them down."

The other two men flanked him from the front and rear, so he was unable to escape. The red-haired one on the back end had his rifle pointed loosely at Cooper's back. The dark short one with the bandaged wrist trudged at the front. Why weren't they riding? Was it the fog?

Victoria looked to Brant, wondering what they could do to help Cooper. Attack the assailants now?

A tendon flicked in Brant's throat. He already had his guns out. He was so slick and quiet on the draw that she hadn't noticed.

Slowly, he brought one revolver up through the pine needles and aimed it at the man holding a gun to Cooper.

Victoria stopped breathing. If Brant missed... She couldn't complete the thought.

She no longer cared about Walker Dixon. She didn't care about any of it. The most vital thing was getting Cooper back to safety.

If Dixon was injured and needed medical attention, let him be the one to suffer, not her friend.

No one could force her to nurse the injuries of a madman. As for the rest of the town of Glitter Mountain, she'd have to devise a plan with the deputy marshal in Skagway for how to safely care for anyone who needed tending. Maybe they could come to her in Skagway.

Or arrange for a slew of bodyguards to protect the next medical team.

The mare behind them moved her foot and snapped a twig. It echoed lightly. Victoria's heart lurched and her eyes widened on the men, praying they'd heard nothing.

The man with the rifle aimed it more directly at Cooper as he swung around to examine the woods, but after a moment, he appeared to see nothing, so he swung back and continued on his way.

Brant and Victoria ducked just as the men passed directly in front of them, but not before Cooper spotted her through the pine needles.

He stumbled for a moment on his feet. He looked directly into her eyes, his expression wild and disbelieving. She froze with fear.

His eyes grew as big as apples, and his lips fell open when his gaze moved to Brant's face.

Brant immediately motioned for Cooper to keep

quiet. Disoriented, Cooper missed his next step, but he quickly picked up the pace and looked to the man behind him for any signs that he'd seen Brant and Victoria, too.

"What's wrong, kid?" said the disheveled man in the back, his thin red hair hanging limp below his cowboy hat. "Pick up that weak leg and walk!"

"Okay, Thorpe," Cooper responded.

The heavyset man at the front, his wrist still bandaged tight with a dirty rag, shouted over his shoulder. "Watch where you're walking!"

"Sorry, Mulroy."

Victoria knew instantly what Cooper was doing. He was giving her and Brant the names of the men.

The wounded monster, Mulroy, muttered, "Should be there any minute."

Victoria frowned at Brant. Where? They should be where?

The next minute happened so quickly she reeled. Brant nodded at her to get down flat to the ground, emphasizing the command by pushing her with a firm hand.

Then he signaled Cooper to drop and roll.

As Cooper did, a bewildered Thorpe stopped shuffling and muttered, "What the hell?"

Brant jumped out of the woods and shouted, "Drop the rifle, Thorpe!"

But Thorpe swung and blasted at Brant.

Brant rolled. The bullet roared through the morning mist, ripping through the fog and thundering through the air. It missed Brant but the explosion startled their mare. She neighed and reared.

Victoria rolled into the far edge of the tall grass so not to get kicked or shot.

Another shot rang out from Mulroy's direction, but Brant was too quick on his feet for either man.

"What the hell ya doin'?" Thorpe hollered. "We'll kill you for this!"

Brant jumped to his feet, and just as Thorpe aimed at him again, Brant shot him in the chest. The man at the front screamed obscenities and pulled his trigger but Brant pivoted and shot him, too. The bullet hit Mulroy's left side and he hit the ground in a pond of blood.

Two men dead.

Cooper rushed to have a look and then, ever grateful, looked long and hard at Brant.

Lying on her stomach, a tide of nausea welling up her throat at the sight of the violence, Victoria dropped her face into her hands. It was over. She trembled. Lord, it was over and she, Brant and Cooper were safe. Two lives had been snuffed out, but God have mercy, they had been criminals and they'd pulled their triggers first.

"Well, well, well," muttered a man coming up

from the trees to her other side, making her jump so high with fright that she snapped some branches.

Defensively, she rolled onto her spine and then reared back at the sight of a gun's barrel six inches from her forehead. The man holding it was roughly thirty, although his slicked-back hair was pure white. He leered at her over a pointy nose and nubby blond cheeks, then yanked her up by the fabric around her throat.

The shock made her heart come to a screeching halt.

"I should kill you for what you just did to my friends."

"No!" Brant's voice pierced the chill.

The man's glare turned from Brant's direction back to her. His seedy eyes shifted past her face, down her body. "What have we got here? Could it be the nurse we've all been waitin' for?"

She froze, like an animal cornered by a predator, gasping for words but not knowing what to say to appease him.

The man kept his barrel pointed at her, but looked up past her head toward the direction of Brant and Cooper again.

"Which one of you's the doctor?"

Not again. Her stomach clenched and the bile came rolling up her throat, threatening to spill.

She heard Brant's big boots shuffle forward and couldn't believe his words. "I am."

Seconds later, Brant itched to slam his fist into the man's throat. But he kept his empty hands in the air, watching and waiting for the grizzled man with the white hair to react.

"We heard about you," he finally uttered, dark eyes darting back and forth from Brant to Cooper.

With a shove, the man released Victoria and she fell back against the moss and grass. Thank God, unharmed, it appeared to Brant.

"Who are you?" Brant asked.

"You'll find out soon enough." He took Brant's guns. "And just in case you're thinking of trying somethin', I got two more friends just up ahead."

"The bottleneck," Brant muttered. He'd thought they were roughly two hours from the mountain pass, but they were closer than he'd thought.

"Ma'am," the scum snarled, "get your things together and join your friends over there. They've got work to do."

At least, Brant thought with some relief, she was getting treated better now that the man knew she was a nurse.

As for himself, he'd take his chances pretending to be a man of medicine.

Cooper didn't say much. Weak and weary, he hobbled around, doing the man's bidding.

"Get the shovels off Mulroy and Thorpe's horses!"

The shovels were small, but they were tools most men carried in this part of the world, just in case something shiny and gold sparkled up from the ground and needed to be investigated.

"You all right?" Brant asked as Victoria came forward.

She nodded, but she was pale and frightened.

Fury pounded through Brant, like a hammer pounding nails. Dixon Walker and all his men were going to pay for this.

He wished now that he'd never taken Victoria with him, that he'd sat back and refused to be her bodyguard.

But then what would've happened? Someone else would be here taking his place, and he didn't trust any other gunman as much as he trusted himself to deal with these outlaws.

His throat tightened with restraint.

The white-haired gunman indicated Brant and Cooper should dig.

More than an hour later, having helped dig two graves at gunpoint, Brant walked along the path with Victoria beside him, Cooper limping behind, and the assailant behind all of them, high atop his mount. The four remaining horses were tethered together behind him. The man with the revolver preferred to keep his three prisoners walking.

They trudged along the grooves of the dirty path. Victoria accidentally brushed Brant's shoulder now and again with her sleeve, but she never let on how difficult this was for her.

She made little eye contact with him and when she did, there was such sorrow reflected there that his outrage hammered through him all over again. But he told himself to temper his anger, to fold it inside of him, to use it to focus on the man behind them and how to maneuver out of this stranglehold.

They walked for roughly three miles before they reached the pass.

Victoria stiffened as they approached the clearing, and two men with rifles drawn slid off their rocky perches. One was an old guy with a nasty beard, the other younger and built as solid as an ox.

It was a paradox, Brant thought, standing among the glorious jagged mountains with the earth and sky stretched before them in all of God's glory, as these stinking vermin come crawling out, somewhere from the bowels of hell.

"Sloan!" the old guy called. "Mulroy and Thorpe with you?"

The white-haired Sloan slid off his saddle and grunted. He slammed the back of his gun between

Brant's shoulder blades. It hit him hard and hurled him forward. "Arrived just in time to see this fella shoot 'em down."

The old guy took a few steps forward, cocking his rifle and pointing it at Brant with a menacing jab. "That right?"

"Before you go shootin' anyone, Eli, beware," Sloan advised him. "He's the doctor Dixon's been waitin' for."

"A doctor with guns?"

Brant spoke up. "How else do you expect me to travel?"

The old guy peered at Victoria. A smile crossed the buzzard's face.

"She's the nurse," Sloan said.

The man known as Eli peered at Cooper. "And the boy?"

"My apprentice," said Brant.

"You don't say," the buzzard growled. "Looks like he belongs in grade school."

"He's just starting out," Brant replied.

The ox, silent till now, heaved one foot in front of the other until he stood a short two feet away from Brant. This monster was a man to be reckoned with.

"Doctor or not, you tell me right now why I shouldn't blast your head off for killin' my friends."

"It was self-defense. They tried to harm my friend, here." Brant pointed to Cooper. "I asked them to drop their weapons but instead, they pulled."

"They've been looking for you for a whole bloody week. Why didn't you identify who you were?"

"We did," Brant lied, trying to make the scene seem like an accidental meeting. "But one of them got spooked and thought Cooper was going for a gun. And as you can see, the boy has no gun."

The ox looked Brant straight in the eye. Neither man flinched.

The ox swung around to Victoria. He stared at her face. After a moment, she looked down at the ground, uncomfortable beneath the scrutiny. Her lips trembled and her chin lost its strength.

"I'm Joshua," the ox told her. "And you're really somethin'." He held out his hand.

Her nostrils flared, she gritted her teeth, then held out her own for a handshake.

Good, thought Brant. *Go along.*

"Dixon's been waitin' for days. What took you?"

"I got…we—we got tied up in Skagway," she stammered.

Brant took over for her, trying to protect her from any wrath by taking it on himself. "We left Skagway late. Couldn't be helped. Medical problems. Then our stagecoach broke down."

Joshua looked to the horses. "You brought medicine?"

"Yeah," said Brant. "It's all there."

Joshua poked his rifle at Cooper's chest. "What have you got to say for yourself, boy?"

Cooper's face started to pound red. It got all blotchy, like Brant had witnessed several times before whenever Cooper got embarrassed. But this time, Cooper fought to catch his breath. In a quick spurt of anger, he banged the rifle off his chest.

Joshua's face clouded over and his lips grew into a thin horizon. Just as Brant braced himself, ready to lunge at the ox, the man chuckled.

"You're like a little rooster. Struttin' for nothin'." He turned to look at his two accomplices. "Let's go."

"Let the lady ride," said Brant.

Joshua swung around, his thick short neck awkwardly twisting as he squinted against the sun. "You're all gonna ride this time."

And so they did. Each of them had a horse. Flanked by the outlaws, Victoria rode first, followed by Cooper and then Brant.

Watchful of any little slip these men might make, Brant kept pace. "How long before we reach Dixon?"

"No talkin'," replied Joshua.

And so they made their way down the canyon.

The fog had lifted. Sunshine warmed Brant's skin. The gentle breeze brought with it a multitude of pleasant mountain scents that he was too preoccupied to fully enjoy—autumn wildflowers, lichen and moss, the smell of the river that wound down from the mountain pass and into the valley of Glitter Mountain. The town sprawled below them, cabins churning out lunchtime smoke, strings of laundry hung on the line—mostly filled with men's underwear and overalls—and then the occasional sighting of chickens, mules and horses.

Straight ahead, a wider cabin came into view. Joshua, at the front, slowed his horse and indicated Victoria do the same. Cooper stopped behind them and Brant rode up beside Victoria.

There was a man standing by a campfire, a hundred yards away from the cabin and ten feet in front of them.

He looked up at Joshua and nodded as he poked at the fire. The man was cooking a meal. Roast venison and boiled coffee. He didn't seem part of this gang, as there was little eye contact between him and the others. The man bowed his head, attentive to his meal.

Brant got the feeling that the man was being forced to cook and didn't like it much.

Victoria snapped her head in Brant's direction, as if wondering what he was thinking.

He wasn't able to explain the significance of the cook's dissatisfaction.

Joshua slid off his mount. He turned around and ordered them off their horses. "One doctor. One apprentice. And one nurse. Finally here."

"Dixon's waitin' for ya inside," said Eli.

Brant slid off his saddle and helped Victoria off hers. She took her medicine bag and he took Cooper's, all shiny and new, and headed toward Walker Dixon's home, pretending to be a doctor.

How the hell was he going to pull this off?

Chapter Sixteen

~~~~~~~~~~~~~~~~~~

Uncertain of what she was walking into, and terrified of the possibilities, Victoria pulled her shoulders back, gripped her medical bag with hot sweaty palms, and followed Brant and Cooper into Dixon's cabin.

She heard the three men behind her slide their guns out of their holsters. Insurance, she supposed, so the medical team would do as they were asked.

How on earth had her life come to this? Only last night, she'd lain in Brant's arms, lost in a blissful night of discovery, daring to dream of love and security and sharing all of life's splendors with him. Not only had that dream faded, but they were now in mortal danger.

She knew what Brant was up to, protecting

Cooper by pretending he was the doctor, and she was awed by the brilliance and boldness of his move. But how on God's green earth was Brant going to give medical aid when he wasn't trained?

He did have a lot of courage. But the thing that ailed her was the possibility that he might lose his life over this.

They all might, if they failed, but he would be first in line.

Inside the cabin, the large room smelled of old tobacco and damp wool bedding.

"About time." A dark figure rose from a chair at the table, its wooden pegs creaking beneath the weight of him. When he looked down at their medical bags, he slid his gun back into his holster.

From the sure way he strolled toward them, the confident manner in which he tilted his scruffy jaw, and how the other men nodded their heads in subservience, she gathered this giant was the boss.

Walker Dixon.

Long black hair hung around his ears. The morning light that spilled from the side window bathed his wide shoulders and heavily muscled thighs. A flash of the fireplace lit the oily skin of his face, the sallow eyes and weak chin.

He wasn't injured, and didn't seem to require medical aid himself.

Then who did?

She looked about the room quickly, but there was no one else in sight. A hallway off the far end, past the fireplace, led around the corner to an area she couldn't see.

"You're Dixon." Brant, clutching Cooper's medical bag, stood without his holster. Never in her born days did she wish more fervently for his guns to appear. The breadth of his shoulders matched Dixon's, but his legs were nowhere near as meaty and muscled.

Dixon was an elephant.

"Yeah," Dixon said, low and threatening. "You must be the doctor." He glowered at Brant, and in that instant, when the elephant reared his head and she caught wind of the rage that made his cheeks tighten and his voice growl, her gut tightened in horror.

Something was wrong.

He was seething. Were they too late for whatever it was he needed them for?

Brant reacted calmly, took his time to answer. "I'm Dr. Cooper Sullivan. What is it you need me for, and why does it have to be at gunpoint?"

"Who are you to talk to me like that?"

"I'm the man with the medicine, remember? And you want me to help you."

The two men, not a yard between them, glared at each other.

Footsteps shuffled around her. Bodies heaved with smelly breathing as the gunmen behind her ringed the room and waited for their orders.

"It's my father," Dixon said between gritted teeth. "He broke his arm."

"In the gold mine. Right," said Brant in a calm manner of efficiency. "I heard."

"You heard." Dixon repeated the words with sarcasm and restrained outrage. Arteries throbbed at his temples. "You were supposed to be here more than two weeks ago."

"Couldn't be helped. Other folks in Skagway needed me."

Dixon gritted his teeth.

Brant's shoulders tensed beneath his jacket and he asked again, "What is it you need?"

"I want you to take a look at him."

"Not until you set the woman free. And the young man."

Dixon snickered. "Is that right? Well, how about this? You look at my pa, and maybe, just maybe, I won't blow this young man's head off."

Cooper shifted his weight, his boots scraping the floor, and stammered, "Let us…let us see him. Let us see your pa."

Victoria was slightly dazed at his brave outburst.

Much as she wanted him to stop and let Brant lead them out of this situation, for he was the trained bounty hunter, Cooper continued. He stood ramrod straight and his stammering left him. "If your pa needs medical help, I assume he needs it fast."

Dixon scoffed and eyed him through narrowed lids. "Who are you, boy?"

"My assistant," Brant intervened.

Dixon turned his eyes from Cooper to her. Her insides crawled with disgust. Her nostrils flared for the stench of this outlaw. But she took her cue from Brant to remain outwardly calm.

"So you're the nurse."

She gulped and nodded.

"And I've got three people to help my pa. Aren't we lucky?"

But he didn't speak like he felt lucky. He was nearly growling and his menacing stance indicated he'd like nothing better than to bash them all against the wall.

Cooper was getting impatient. And too daring for his own good. He stepped out toward Dixon, half the man's weight, a fly next to an elephant.

Cooper said it again. "Do you want help or not, mister?"

Brant lifted his hand protectively to Cooper's chest. "Andy," Brant said calmly, eyeing Cooper and giving him a false name. "Easy now. Let me handle this."

Dixon took out his gun, stepped up to Cooper and cocked the hammer at his face.

Victoria caught her breath.

If he was intending to shoot, Dixon changed his mind. "You first, boy. Down that hall."

Victoria whispered a prayer beneath her breath. Cooper went first, then Brant, then her. Dixon's footsteps thudded behind her. She could feel his eyes on the back of her head, her shoulders, her hips.

She wished she had a gun.

As soon as she passed the popping and sizzling sounds of the fireplace, she heard the raspy breathing. And there, around the corner past the log wall, a man lay on a narrow cot, hacking in his sleep. Tall, white-haired and grimy, he hadn't been bathed in weeks. He wore long johns, ripped at the sleeve to expose his bandaged, broken arm.

Even from her distance, six feet away, Victoria could see his condition didn't look good. The bandaged limb was swollen and crooked along the upper arm, where the break obviously was, and the gauze they'd wrapped it with was caked in dried blood and pus. Gangrene was highly likely.

She groaned audibly and stopped in her tracks.

Dried blood stained the floor. It was smeared, as if someone had tried to wipe it. The bedding had a few blotches of blood, too. And the wall had some splatters.

What had happened here? Good Lord.

Suddenly, she understood the misplaced rage of the man behind her. His father was the poor man on the bed, and the broken arm was too deeply infected to save. The limb likely would have to be amputated, otherwise the festering would spread through the bloodstream and take his life.

Even if she had gotten here sooner, it still might have festered and might have needed to be amputated at some point, if this filthy bed was any indication of the squalid conditions of care.

It wasn't her fault, nor Cooper's, nor any medical personnel, if gangrene had set in. They didn't have medicine to prevent it. Cleanliness of the bedding and personal hygiene were the only defenses.

Dixon planted his heavy fingers into her lower spine and pushed her forward.

"Take a good look and see what you did."

He poked her shoulder blades with the barrel of his gun and she fell onto Brant. He whipped around at Dixon to retaliate, but she stood in Brant's way and shook her head. He'd only be shot. There had to be a better time for them to try to escape.

Brant and Victoria turned and edged closer to the bed. The man drew in a croak of a breath, saturated with the smell of whiskey. He had a fever, obvious from the sweat on his forehead. Maybe he was sleeping, but maybe he was unconscious from pain.

Brant planted his medical bag on the straw mattress.

"When was the bandage last changed?" she asked.

"Don't recall."

"We need to unwind it to have a look," said Cooper. "See how far the germs have spread."

So Cooper had noticed it, too, she thought, and he also suspected gangrene. In fact, the odor was giving away the arm's condition.

"What did you give him for pain?" Victoria asked.

She, Cooper and Brant swung around to look at Dixon for an answer.

His lashes flicked at Brant, as if Dixon was wondering why the other two were doing the talking for the doctor. "Whiskey. But now that you're here, you'll give him something stronger. Something proper."

"Absolutely," said Brant.

Dixon's eyes glimmered at Brant with a dangerously quiet edge, making her pulse vibrate with terror.

"We'll give him some…some morphine," said Brant. "Who did the bandaging?" He was merely guessing at the questions he should be asking if he was truly a doctor, thought Victoria.

"The cook standing outside."

"He did a fine job controlling the bleeding," said Cooper with no hesitation, again surprising her with his quick and even response.

"Oh, real fine job," snapped Dixon. "Couldn't have gone smoother."

Brant unbuckled Cooper's medical bag as if he knew what he was doing. "I'll…I'll give him that shot."

Cooper lunged for the bag. "Let me get that for you, Doctor."

Brant shifted his gaze to Victoria and secretly nodded at the bed. What was he getting at?

She peered closer and saw it. There was a revolver close to the old man's hand, tucked into the sheets on the right side of the bed. The man might be sleeping, or unconscious and unable to reach for his gun, but they had to move carefully.

There was no sense taking the gun themselves, for they weren't sure if it was loaded. And with the army standing behind them, Brant would be a goner before he even pulled the trigger.

Brant nodded openly at her. "Nurse, I'd rather you draw it up."

Yes, thought Victoria, she was more capable than Cooper. She took a step toward the bag, her skirts skimming the floor planks, squeezing herself between Brant and Cooper.

"No, I insist," said Cooper, pushing his way to the bag.

What was he doing? Where was he getting this inner strength? His voice was calm, but for God's sake, he was sweating. His temples were drenched and his upper lip was trembling. He would give them away.

He nudged her hands aside and searched through his leather compartments, his hands as steady as she'd ever seen them. But his trademark red blotches came crawling up his cheeks, giving away his fear.

Would he give the old man something else?

Lord, no, she prayed. Give the man morphine. He might be a criminal as nasty and unremorseful as his son, but he was still a wounded man.

She watched Cooper open a vial of the correct medicine, thank goodness, and reach for a needle and glass syringe. The old man on the bed began to moan and shake, startling her and taking Dixon's eyes off them for a moment to look at his pa.

Cooper took the few seconds to reach into the bag, lift a secret leather compartment and reveal the handle of a revolver to Brant.

A gun. Blazes, he had a hidden gun, thought Victoria. That's why he wanted to draw up the syringe. To show Brant the gun.

Then as quickly as the gun had appeared, it disappeared again beneath the folds, and Cooper finished drawing up the morphine.

"Give it to him," Dixon bellowed. "Dammit, he's in a lotta pain. Give it to him!"

Cooper handed Brant the syringe, then Cooper reached over the sleeping man, yanked the torn underwear down over the shoulder of the good arm to expose the bicep, and rolled a dab of antiseptic solution on it.

Smoothly, Brant took the syringe, held it firmly and plunged the needle into the muscle Cooper had cleared off. Cooper was brilliant in how he'd guided Brant without detection.

"He'll be sleepy for a few hours," said Brant. "We gave him a stiff dose. When it kicks in, my assistant and I will unwind the bandaging and have a look." Brant straightened. "But he also needs something else."

Dixon eyed him with suspicion. "What?"

"Clean bedding. Fresh air."

"Fresh air?"

"Yeah. Lying in this filth is contributing to his poor health."

"Shut your damn mouth. You better save his arm."

Brant nodded slightly and didn't argue.

Dixon growled, "Think you can?"

Brant didn't show a moment's weakness. "Yes."

What was he saying? They likely couldn't save it at all.

But Dixon nodded in relief, buying the answer.

"But," Brant added, "you've got to wash his sheets and let the sun shine on his face."

"What are you gettin' at?"

"Sunshine is a big healer. Everyone needs fresh air to breathe better."

Dixon looked down at his father. The side of his mouth puckered, and he frowned as if contemplating the right course of action.

"That's right," said Victoria. "You'd want it, wouldn't you? If you were in his place? You'd want out of that bed."

Dixon's eyes pivoted to her face again, and queasiness rolled up her throat. She waited and waited for the elephant to respond, while she hoped and prayed he'd give them a way out of this cabin and away from the point-blank barrels of the guns the three silent men behind them were holding, waiting for permission to shoot.

A moment later, Dixon gave the nod to his men to lift the narrow bed, roughly a yard wide, and carry his father outside. Brant walked past Dixon, clenching his right fist, ready to pound the bloody killer in the face. One quick slug would stun the brute, giving Brant enough time to draw the man's Colt and turn it back on him.

But it would also put Victoria and Cooper straight in the line of fire from the other gunmen.

So Brant forced his knuckles to remain still, forced himself to swallow his pride and his fury at being trapped, and forced himself to follow Cooper and Victoria out the cabin door in brewing silence.

He was still holding on to the medical bag, and he thumbed the unclasped buckle. The revolver was only inches away, but how could he get at it without being spotted and gunned down first?

He thought of the answer as he stepped out onto the front porch and clambered down behind Victoria. The cook he'd seen earlier at the fire, wearing a single gun strapped to his thigh, was watering the horses at the far trough by the small barn. There were six horses, untied and ready for the taking.

All Brant needed was three.

He swung around to stare at the others as Cooper and Victoria came to stand beside him. With a nod and a lift of his shoulder, he indicated the horses by the trough.

Slyly, Victoria turned around to look and quickly turned back to him. Her lips fell open as if unsure what he meant, maybe the timing of it all, but Cooper nodded in response.

Atta boy. Cooper was ready.

Dixon stepped onto the front porch, wielding his gun, followed by two of his henchmen who were carrying the bed, along with the sleeping old man on top of it, out the door. The third gunman, the white-haired one, was somewhere behind the bed, still in the cabin.

"Hey, Sloan," grumbled one of the men, heaving beneath the weight of the cot as he reached the wide door opening. "Give me a hand here. It's got to tilt to the right slightly so we can get it out the door."

And that's when the old man on the bed made his move. The morphine must've kicked in for pain relief. And either he felt himself slipping slightly on the bed, or the turning gave him a jolt, for he jerked awake, grabbed his gun, lifted it in Victoria's direction and blasted.

She shrieked as Brant jumped on top of her. The bullet zinged past his ear as he yanked open the medicine bag and ripped out the gun, screaming at Victoria and Cooper. "Run!"

Her skirts kicked up the dust and Cooper's boots churned up pebbles as Dixon fired in their direction.

Brant hit the ground and fired at Dixon at the same time the brute aimed at him. A bullet hit Dixon's leg. He fell.

"Goddamn!"

The old man on the bed tried firing again, but the men dropped his bed, wedging it between the door and the porch, so none of them could get out. Sloan, in a fit of rage, jumped on top of the mattress and lunged through the door after Brant.

Brant rolled on the grass again, looked to Victoria and Cooper, who'd each found a horse, much to the dismay of the cook.

"Stop it!" the cook yelled. "Stop it!" But the man wasn't going for his gun.

Obviously, he wasn't part of this gang. And his gun was useless to him all this time because Dixon's men would've shot him cold if he'd so much as lifted the gun toward them.

Brant rolled to one knee, then raced through the trees as the sole gunman, Sloan, blasted his weapon. A bullet nicked Brant's ear but he kept running toward freedom.

He heard Dixon shout out, "Pa! Pa! Don't try to get up!"

Victoria's horse reared in the commotion. The cook dove for the ground.

Cooper swung around on his reins, waiting for Brant, circling toward him and holding out the reins of the third horse. The other horses circled, jittery and scared at the commotion.

"Come on," Cooper yelled. "Take the reins! Come on!"

Brant charged at them, running flat out as fast he could, half hidden by the trees, but two bullets zipped past his shoulders toward Cooper and Victoria. They were straight in the line of fire because of him.

"Go," he screamed, doubling back and running away from them. "Ride!"

"Not without you!" Victoria's horse was hard to handle and it reared a second time.

Brant changed directions again and reached Cooper, shielded now by one of the other horses, and slapped the rear end of his mare. "Go!"

The mare bucked and tore off as Brant did the same to Victoria's mount. "Ride! Ride!"

The roan whinnied and Victoria shouted, "Brant!"

But to his relief, both horses tore off like hellfire through the woods, leaving him in the dust.

They got away and now it was his turn.

He jumped onto a palomino, just as he heard the click of a gun at his side. With heart pounding, he stared down into the eyes of the trembling cook.

"If I don't stop you," the man panted between trembling lips, "they're gonna kill me."

Chapter Seventeen

With barely time to think, Brant leaped off the horse and jumped onto the cook with such force it flattened the man to the ground and knocked the wind out of him. The palomino galloped away as Brant grabbed the man's revolver from his hand.

With Dixon and his men now yards away, blocked by jittery and rearing horses, Brant hit the dirt, rolled to the woods and over the edge of the cliff.

"Get him!" Dixon shouted.

Gunfire blasted around his ears but Brant kept running, bouncing among the trees. His ear was bleeding down to his collar, but he barely felt the sting as he stretched every muscle in his thighs to slide down moss, roots and boulders. His pants ripped at the knee. His jacket sleeve tore on a branch.

A bullet grazed his left shoulder but it didn't penetrate the muscle. Just enough to rip the skin and cause another patch of blood to seep against the suede.

He heard the scrape of boots far above him, looked up and tried to identify the man, a dark blur through the trees. Brant's heartbeat raced so loud he could hear it pounding in his ears. Who was the man? How many guns did he have?

Brant turned his head to look down below, toward the gully. A cabin appeared in view. Then two or three others. He flew behind a tree, nestled himself between the branches and aimed up at the assailant chasing him.

Hell. It was the cook. Brant knew he was unarmed, since Brant had his gun, but the man might be carrying something else.

The cook screamed, "Don't shoot! I've got bullets for you!"

Was he bluffing?

Just to be certain, Brant kept his sights on the man till he got up close. Then without a doubt of his sincerity, the cook withdrew a handful of bullets that ringed his holster and flung them at Brant.

"You'll need these."

Brant shoved them into his pockets.

Three of Dixon's men were charging from above, jumping from tree to tree, bullets blazing, followed by Dixon himself, limping from his wound. He'd tied a scarf around the injured bottom part of his leg. Brant's earlier shot couldn't have gone too deep, or Dixon wouldn't be following at all.

Four against two. But then, as the cook emptied the last of his bullets and threw them at Brant, he tore off down the hill, abandoning him.

Four against one.

Brant looked up at the top of the ridge. What was that…? He squinted. Hell. Dixon's father held a gun.

Five against one.

Brant raised his weapon but it was hard to aim between the wall of trees.

He aimed carefully, slowly, at the outlaw with the slicked-back white hair. He squeezed the trigger and hit the man in the chest.

Bulls-eye. One down.

Footsteps thudded behind Brant. He ducked and wheeled around as the man, a friend, blasted double barrels up toward Dixon's men at the ridge.

"Dammit," Brant said, recognizing the scarred left cheek. "John Abraham. Where the hell have you been?"

"Couldn't get through the pass till Dixon's men left it."

Then another man appeared in the woods behind John.

Another. And another.

Brant stood in awe. The whole town of Glitter Mountain was coming out against Dixon and his men.

"They've got a lot of enemies," Brant said to John, aiming carefully at Dixon as he hid behind brush.

John hit one of the henchmen. Dixon saw it, and the coward in him, rather than helping, fled the man's side. He made a break for it behind the boulders of the gully, toward the more populated area of cabins.

Brant lifted his barrel, taking aim, but in the end couldn't fire for fear of hitting a cabin or an innocent stranger.

Brant leaned toward John. "Take care of these men. I'm going after Dixon."

With a leap, Brant took cover behind the shrubs and trees. He crawled on his knees in the open patch of grass and with a heave, rolled onto the pebbly surface of dirt at the side of the cabin Dixon had disappeared behind.

Had he gone inside?

Crouched down low beside the wall of the cabin, Brant quickly reloaded his revolver and listened for signs of life. There was moaning inside. Sounded like a wounded animal. A woman's voice raised in hysteria.

If Dixon was inside, Brant couldn't hear him.

Slowly, he peered around the edge of the cabin to look as the front door creaked open.

A woman peered out, her face scrunched in fright. Dressed in a red satin gown that was half torn and stained, she was apparently a painted lady. She seemed young and pretty beneath it all, with long black hair.

She sobbed into her hand, then turned around and went back inside. When she turned, Brant was so shocked to see how bruised and swollen her face was that he stopped to stare for a second.

In that second, someone knocked his head from behind. His head pounded but he kept his hold on his gun and rolled.

Dixon kicked it out of his hand so hard with the power behind those elephant legs that he bent two of Brant's fingers back. Brant cursed him.

"Now," Dixon bellowed, "it's your turn—"

Before the man could get his words out, Brant charged like a bull at the elephant's weak spot—his knees.

Dixon thundered to the ground. Beyond the cabins, bullets flew into trees as the rest of the men were preoccupied with their own battles.

Brant pummeled Dixon's hard gut. Dixon's gun went flying.

"Uh," he groaned, then squirmed and smashed the left side of Brant's head with a flat rock.

Dazed, Brant closed his eyes for a moment. He heard the man rise up to his full height, lunging about for more rocks to lift, but Brant rolled and jumped to his feet.

Blood trickled down his temple and that side of his head pounded with pain. His eyesight went wobbly in his left eye, but it only served to infuriate him.

With a shout, he leaped for Dixon and smashed his face with both fists.

The man crumpled to his knees, blood dripping from his nose, and attempted to go for the remaining gun in his holster. Brant reached it first and slid it out.

Heaving to catch his breath, Brant took a step back, gun aimed at Dixon.

Dixon, too, was panting for air, sliding his thick fingers along his upper lip to catch the blood spilling from his nose.

"I'm taking you in," Brant gasped between breaths. His ribs ached, his temple pounded and his grazed shoulder stung like hell.

The cool wind of Alaska cleared the air between them. Gunshots were dying down on the cliffs.

Someone was winning, and Brant hoped like hell it was his side. The cabin where the woman had come out sat quiet.

"Like hell you are," huffed Dixon.

"For the cold-blooded murder of seventeen men. Ranging in age from nineteen to fifty-eight, in twelve states and territories."

Dixon, rising to his thick legs, sneered. "I believe your count is off."

"Dead or alive," Brant snarled. "You pick."

Ten feet away and now standing on his feet, a massive beast of a man, Dixon glared at Brant, then lowered his sights to the gun.

Slowly, maybe finally seeing the futility of his situation, Dixon lifted those hairy hands upward in surrender. But then in a quick jerky movement, his right hand moved over his shoulder as if he was going for a hidden weapon behind him.

One shot rang out from behind Dixon.

He slumped forward. His eyes opened wide in horror, realizing he'd been shot, and then he crumpled to the dirt, face first.

Behind him, holding the smoking gun, stood the painted young lady, ragged hair blowing around her face, torn dress and one eye bruised up so bad it couldn't open fully.

"Dead," she said. "His choice."

Dixon's chest stopped moving and his breath left him.

Brant stepped over his body, saw the knife he'd tucked in his belt, and went to the woman to comfort her. Whatever torment she'd been in, it was over.

Dixon was dead.

Twenty minutes later when all the gunfire had ceased and Victoria finally located Brant, she gasped in alarm at his condition. He was leaning against the front stoop of a cabin, removing his torn jacket and tending to his wounded shoulder. The left side of his head was matted with blood.

"Thank you, Lord," she whispered. He was alive.

She raced among the strangers—folks who'd come to help defeat the outlaw gang—to Brant's side. Her legs shook as she reached him.

"God," she breathed, "you're safe."

"Victoria." He flew to embrace her, crushing her against his chest, holding her as if believing he'd never see her again. "How'd you get here? What happened?"

"John Abraham found us and brought us back. Are you all right? Let me look at your head."

A lump the size of her palm was already swelling above his ear. The cut didn't look very deep, but it would need to be cleaned and she didn't have supplies.

"I've called for my medical bag," she said. "Someone's gone up the ridge to get it."

"Yeah," he said, not able to get enough of watching her. She felt his eyes upon her as she pushed back his hair to get a better look at his scalp. He winced but allowed her touch.

She looked lower to his bloody ear. A bullet had nicked the edge, nothing serious, although the bleeding was heavy. It had dribbled down his neck and saturated his collar. His sleeve was shredded from a bullet blast, too, and she needed to wipe the blood.

She looked up past the cabin. Where was her bag?

And how on earth, she thought as her throat tightened in sympathy, was she to help him if she had no supplies?

"It's all right," he murmured, catching her by the elbow, insisting she sit beside him. "It's all right. Superficial wounds. I'll be okay."

But he looked horrible, all covered in blood like this, and she'd nearly lost him.

Cooper raced up behind the group standing around Dixon's body. "Brant! Brant!"

"Yeah," he responded.

"Oh, bloody hell, you're still standing. Sitting."

Cooper tried to stifle a loud sob but it came blathering out anyway. His eyes watered and he turned away for a minute.

"It's all right," Brant assured him. "It's over. They got the others on the ridge, too. All dead. Dixon. His father. Everyone."

Cooper rubbed his eyes with the sleeve of his jacket. "His father, too? You sure?"

Brant nodded. "Yeah, but not before the old man lodged a bullet into a neighbor's elbow."

Victoria winced. So much bloodshed for the sake of one gang. How many other victims had they taken, who hadn't been lucky enough to have others helping them?

Others like Brant.

Cooper peered past the cabin toward the gully. "Here come our supplies." He took his medical bag from one of the men, handed Victoria hers and looked to the crowd. He nodded to the painted lady, by the name of Maria, who was tightly clutching a shawl and answering questions from John Abraham.

Someone had given John a leaf of stiff paper, and he was jotting down a few notes and getting witnesses to sign them.

Cooper flagged her over as he explained. "The lady in the red dress says her brother's inside with a broken foot. I'll go see to him." He strode away. "Maria!"

She came toward him, and they hopped over the front stoop Victoria and Brant were sitting on. Then they disappeared into the log cabin.

Victoria touched Brant's sleeve, looking in awe at the closed cabin door. "He went inside by himself."

Brant nodded.

Her eyes misted. "He's going to make a fine doctor."

Brant nodded. He was silent, too, as if aware of the significance.

"You made him face it," she said. "With Dixon's father up on the ridge, you pulled it out of Cooper."

"I had very little to do with it." Brant peered at the trees and watched two dogs run by. His voice wobbled with emotion. "Seems like Cooper finally decided what he wants to do with his life."

Holding back a wave of sentiment herself, Victoria nodded. She was overwhelmed by Cooper's fearlessness, Brant's loyalty and the injuries he'd sustained. Wiping away the moistness from her cheeks, she unbuckled her bag and looked for her antiseptic bottle.

"What about you, Victoria?" Brant asked with a low rumble. "Have you decided about your life?"

It tore her in two to have to face what was in her

heart. "When I thought I'd lost you…" She soaked her gauze bandages and cleaned his head wound. He flinched at the sting. "I wasn't sure how I'd go on."

"You didn't lose me, though."

"I think you're the bravest man I've ever known, and will likely ever know in my lifetime."

He touched her hand. She stumbled slightly at the heat between them, then forced herself to go on cleansing and go on talking.

"I understand now…the type of people you face when you go after someone like Dixon."

He swallowed hard. Lines of emotion bit into his cheeks.

"Someone's got to do it," she whispered, repeating what he'd once told her. "Alaska's young. The district barely has a lawman in Skagway, let alone deputies and surrogates who can patrol the land. It's worse than most places." She dabbed his bloody ear. "And if it were me…if it were someone I loved who they'd injured or killed, I'd want you fighting for me. I'd be the most blessed person on earth if I had you on my side."

He stiffened, as if he knew what was coming.

"But I can't live like this, Brant." Her throat was raw and tight. "Not like this. This is who you are. But it's not who I am."

Chapter Eighteen

Brant couldn't blame Victoria for how she felt, but it didn't make her words any easier to take.

Later that evening, he was still trying to recover from their conversation as he unsaddled his horse outside the cabins where they would spend the night. The cook who'd escaped Dixon's clutches had arranged it for them. Victoria and Cooper were inside, washing up. John Abraham was seeing to it that the dead were buried and that eyewitness accounts were written down for the records. Across the road, some folks were sitting on their porches watching Brant, while other neighbors were going over all the details of the gunfight, blow-by-blow.

Brant's mare ate from the feeding trough as he brushed her coat. There was something simple and rewarding in taking care of a horse. It brought him stability where he was faltering.

Victoria had said what was on her mind and in her heart. She likely couldn't control her feelings any more than he could control his.

He hadn't seen her in five years and it was only a slip of circumstances that he'd bumped into her in Alaska.

Could she have said things any plainer? She couldn't accept him for who he was and what he did for a living.

At least he could thank her for that. She was a woman who didn't mince words, and why torture himself for thinking what might have been?

His mind urged him to remain logical and see the situation for what it was—a lady he'd been attracted to no longer cared for his company. But his heart felt as though someone had stitched the ends with a needle and was tugging hard.

Voices from around the corner got louder. Brant turned to look. John broke from a crowd and came walking over to Brant's side.

John shoved his notes into the pocket of his leather coat. "The outlaws each had a price on their heads."

"I'm aware," Brant told him, running a hand over the soft coat of the mare.

"Including Dixon's old man."

"I realize that, too. Didn't know he'd be here, though. It was difficult to get the facts straight without seeing it all myself."

"I'm not sure how the bounty will be divided, but without you, none of this would've gone down. I figure it's yours, Brant. Up to the deputy marshal when we get back to Skagway, but he'll go along with the witnesses here."

Brant looked over the shoulders of his horse to John. He was a good man. Brant had sensed it from the moment they'd shook hands weeks ago in Skagway, when they'd first met. He was a straight shooter, both with his words and his gun. Honest. Treated people fairly. That's why the deputy marshal counted on him in times like these. John was a trail guide and sharpshooter when needed, and Brant wouldn't mind working with him again sometime.

Brant went back to brushing. "The town can have the bounty. I believe Dixon's reward should go to Maria."

Abraham squinted in the fading sun. "You sure?"

"Yeah." Brant didn't need the money; he was well established. Nor did he want it this time. The fact that these killers had been stopped was what mattered. "Seeing how the whole town had come out to help me overpower Dixon and his men, they earned it."

John nodded, took out his notes and wrote it

down. He handed Brant the paper for his signature, and Brant obliged.

Just as they were finishing up, ten yards away, the door of the big cabin opened with a squeak. Cooper came out, followed by Victoria.

She peered over at Brant, clutching the worn lapel of her duster against the cut of her cheekbone, her eyes finding his then looking away quickly. Was this how it was going to be? A silent connection they were both supposed to ignore. The cool wind lifted the collar of his jacket and ruffled his hair, giving him a chill.

"Ma'am," said John with respect as the two approached. "Cooper."

"How's Maria's brother?" Brant asked Cooper.

"Fever's gone. Broken bones in his feet might not mend perfectly, but he'll be able to walk again." Cooper, his hair slicked back and parted, thumbed his belt and glanced toward Maria's cabin. Smoke poured out of its chimney. "Maria had the foresight to keep his wound clean, and changed the soiled bandaging on a regular basis."

"Good to hear." Brant patted his horse's nose and looked to Victoria. "And how's Maria?"

Victoria took a step closer to Cooper's side, her skirts fanning the ground. "Still traumatized from all that's happened." She met Brant's eyes this time and he felt a stirring of emotions, a longing so deep and raw it made his gut ache. "But she…she cleaned up and looks a lot better. She'll be all right, too."

Brant ran his brush down the muscled back of the horse, grateful he had something to divert his attention away from Victoria. It was easier dealing with a horse than it was dealing with her.

"You did a fine job," he said to his companions.

"When you're a doctor," said Cooper, "you can't sit in judgment of a man's life. You gotta help them all the same. Maybe that's what you taught me in that cabin back there, with the elder Mr. Dixon."

The assessment was so mature and wise that Brant looked over at Victoria again. Her cheeks pulled up with pride and her lips parted with a certainty he'd never seen before. They'd all changed on this trip.

All of them. Cooper had grown from a young lad who wasn't sure of what he wanted out of life, to a man well on his way to becoming a skilled doctor. He'd surely seen and done more in his three months of practice here in Alaska with Victoria than all his colleagues put together back in Philadelphia.

As for Brant, he'd seen the cost of loving and losing a woman he hadn't expected to ever see again.

And Victoria… She'd seen a softer part of him that maybe she thought didn't exist.

Well, it did exist. That tender side of him he fought so hard to hide. And where had it gotten him?

Nowhere.

He gritted his jaw, tightened his resolve to never show that side of himself again, and went back to tending to his horse.

The conversation continued between John, Victoria and Cooper, but Brant stayed out of it. Just as he did for the next few days as they headed back to Skagway. No sense stirring up his heart by going anywhere near her. It just hurt too much.

They'd been on the road for three days, and Brant was still keeping to himself. Victoria rolled over in her bedroll and studied the red embers of the fire. Orange flames swirled in the light wind. The glow saturated her cheeks and the front of her blanket. A flake of snow drifted from the top of the trees.

Brant was lying on the other side of the fire, Cooper closest to her head and John by her feet. Tomorrow, they'd meet up with Gus and tell him their story. She prayed he was fine, that his ankle had healed, and that they'd find him safe and well with the two Finch brothers.

What would she say to Gus?

Good to see you, friend, and did you know Brant and I were involved the whole time we were on this trip? Even if she hadn't realized it at first, every minute since she'd boarded that stagecoach, they were in each other's thoughts and expectations. Except that it had ended, and she would've been far better off if they hadn't silently connected in the first place.

Then she wouldn't be second-guessing herself every time he avoided her gaze, every time he spoke to Cooper and not her, and every time he filleted a fish or threw a rabbit onto the fire and she was forced to gaze at those long firm fingers that had once held her against his body.

Another log crumbled. The rush of fire as it scorched the underbelly of wood made a rushing sound in the air, masking whatever insects and birds were here with them tonight.

She missed his arms looping around her waist. She missed the feel of his lips on hers, the scent of his skin and the touch of his hand on her breast.

She sighed and buried her face into the pile of blankets.

Brant, I want you.

Brant, I know you're not sleeping.

Brant, why can't you be what I need?

Her feelings went deeper than anything she'd ever felt for a man. A thousand times more than what she'd felt for Martin. And a thousand times more frustrating, too.

Why couldn't he leave his job? Weren't his feelings for her stronger than his desire to chase criminals to justice?

Then guilt set in, weaving its shaky ribbons around her throat and squeezing it to finally make her exhale in discomfort. Who was she to tell him how to live his life? Who was she to make him walk away from helping folks in dire need?

Nobody.

He'd resent her if she forced him.

And that was no way to live the rest of her life.

Besides, he wasn't even asking her for a commitment of any kind. This was all in her head. The unspoken thought of a possible future life together that neither of them thought possible any longer. If they did, they'd be in each other's arms right now, and not lying ten feet away with their faces turned to everything and everyone but each other.

She closed her eyes again to the heat of the fire and listened to the flames dance across the logs. They skipped and fell and sizzled, until she finally found solace in darkness.

Bouncing with joy at seeing the stagecoach driver she'd grown so attached to, Victoria fought to catch her breath.

"Gus Newly! We've been looking all over for you!" Brant shouted into the noon sunshine as she and Cooper raced behind to catch up with the old man as he fished by the river.

The Finch brothers stood beside him at the swirling green water, and all three raised their heads in unison.

"Son of a gun," Gus shouted. He dropped his fishing pole and came to stand beside them.

Victoria gave the big man a hug, pleased to see he'd lost most of his limp and looked well rested.

Gus held his hand out to Cooper. "I see you got the young man back."

"Yes, sir," Cooper replied.

Victoria looked proudly at Cooper. Everything about him seemed stronger and more independent—his sure stance, his choice of words, the way he carried his medical bag as if it was part of him now and not an awkward nuisance.

"What happened?" Gus asked them.

"We made it to Glitter Mountain," said Brant, patting the old man on the shoulders and beaming as broadly as she was to see him safe.

"Lots of folks need your help?"

"It's a long story." Brant inhaled and nodded to the Finch brothers as they brought their fishing poles along and headed toward their cabin.

"Share some lunch with us," said the younger, clean-shaven one.

"Much obliged," said Victoria. "How's the arm?"

"Better."

They took their supplies inside while Brant answered questions, and every now and again Victoria took a turn, too. Their journey home wasn't taking nearly as long as their initial one because no medical calls needed to be made. Yet the time seemed to pass so much more slowly, as she and Brant fought to avoid each other.

Gus eyed her from the table as they ate a hearty stew, then looked to Brant, who kept his distance from her by sitting at the other end of the table.

It was embarrassing, for even Cooper seemed aware there was something wrong between them.

Two days ago he'd asked point-blank, "You all right? What's going on between you and Brant?"

"Nothing," she'd told him, for she couldn't very well confide everything to Cooper. "We're both just tired from the events."

Yesterday, he'd asked, "Don't tell me there's nothing going on. I can see it."

"We'll be fine as soon as we get back to Skagway. Spending too much time together, that's all."

Cooper had bought the excuses initially, but now his mouth flinched and he frowned whenever the two of them avoided each other.

It didn't matter, for she wasn't about to explain herself to anyone. She'd much rather forget the entire journey.

She tried to for the remaining four days. The Finch brothers had been kind enough to extract the stagecoach from the mud, using their own mules, and wheel it back to their cabin. Now, Brant and Gus and Cooper hitched their horses to the lines, and they all waved goodbye to the Finch brothers.

They headed home. Brant sat up front with Gus most of the time, while she and Cooper shared the interior. John rode in the saddle, and led the extra horse back to Skagway. The spare had belonged to Dixon, but the town had gladly given it to Victoria so that they'd each have their own horse on their way to catching up to Gus. The townsfolk had told her they hoped she'd come back next spring on one of her medical calls.

She hadn't made up her mind on anything yet.

However, as she rode in the coach, she knew what Brant was up to, leaving her alone back here. Despite the slight of his turning his back on her, she was gratified that she didn't have to squeeze herself in beside him, possibly with knees knocking and suffering through those uncomfortable glances.

She thanked the Lord when they pulled up to Colburne Stables in Skagway early one morning.

Cooper hopped out first, and even though Brant had opened the door for her, Cooper held out his hand to her to disembark.

"Thank you," she said, cupping her fingers in his and nodding to Brant as though they were strangers.

"I'll get your trunk and your bags," Brant told her, "and have them delivered to your home. The first boardinghouse on the right side, past the clinic, you said?"

She nodded. Was this it, then?

"Thank you for...for getting us home safely, Brant." Her chin wavered.

His nostrils flared and he twisted his bottom lip as though he had more to say. She waited for a moment, but that was all. She'd see him again, though. He was staying in Skagway at least for the winter, she'd overheard him telling Gus.

"Miss Windhaven," said John, removing his hat, "thank you for your company."

She barely had time to respond when a whirl of men came barreling out of the stables, hollering their greetings and asking how it went in Glitter Mountain.

When the men caught wind that a gang of out-laws had been captured, they responded with a downpour of questions. Brant, especially, got stuck in the middle of the crowd, explaining. John, too.

Brant wasn't even looking her way anymore.

Cooper held out his elbow toward her. "Shall we?"

She was grateful to escape the crowd and unable

to control the mounting emotions she had for Brant any longer. They were through and though she thought it was for the best, she couldn't stem the disappointment she felt.

Victoria gave Gus a goodbye kiss on the cheek and slipped her gloved hand into Cooper's arm. They headed down the boardwalk toward her boardinghouse.

Brant likely hadn't even noticed she was leaving.

Lord, it was good to be back in Skagway. The first thing she'd do was wash up and run to the clinic to see how her friends were doing and who in town had gotten ill while she'd been away. She'd tell them all about her trip—save for the personal interludes with Brant—and like the good friends they were, they'd sympathize with the hardships and rejoice with the successes.

"Victoria?" Cooper squeezed her hand tighter into the crux of his elbow.

A few flakes of snow drifted past his face. She squeezed her collar tighter, trying to keep warm from the wind that was whipping down from the icy mountains, but the shiver wouldn't leave her.

"Yes, Cooper?"

"That was quite a trip, wasn't it?"

"Yes, it was. And you can be very proud of how you handled everything."

"I've got you to thank for that."

"It was you and not—"

"Thank you," he insisted, his clear eyes sparkling with warmth.

She smiled and nodded in acceptance.

With his bowler hat, his string tie swinging from his collar, he even seemed to walk differently now.

"I must have seemed like a bit of a coward when you first met me," he said as they walked past the shops. "Never wanting to help much."

"I...I never really noticed." What else could she say? There was no sense hurting his feelings.

"'Course you did. You're just being polite. And that's why...that's why I appreciate you so much, Victoria."

A lump bobbed in her throat. Cooper had found his way to love medicine.

"You'll write to me, then?" she asked.

Cooper's light blue eyes caught the sun and she saw something much deeper and gentler than she'd seen on the trip. It brought a rush of fear to her stomach. Oh, no, those feelings of his that Brant had once brought to her attention.

He's sweet on you, Brant had said.

Was she reading Cooper correctly? Or was this another one of those moments she wasn't sure of? Like so many confusing others she'd had on this trip.

"I'd like to do more than write." His voice was

decisive. "Philadelphia's a long way from here. But you must miss it. Not Philadelphia precisely, because you've never been there. But the city, I mean. You must miss that. Store shops. Proper schools. An endless supply of medicines and equipment. You'd never need to ask for anything in Philadelphia."

"Oh, Cooper…"

"I'd provide it. I'd like to provide it all for you. You're brilliant, Victoria. You'd make a fine nurse for any doctor wishing for the best assistant. And more."

"Cooper…please…"

"I'm wishing," he murmured, turning to look down into her eyes. "I'm wishing for the best. For you, Victoria."

She knew what he was asking. She knew by the sincerity in his voice and the shakiness of his bottom lip. She sought to hide her own tremors, the quake in her legs and the catch in her throat.

Gently, he leaned over and, as light as the snowflakes dancing around them, kissed her cheek.

"Come with me to Philadelphia, Victoria. As my wife."

Chapter Nineteen

More than a week had passed since they'd arrived home to Skagway, and Brant was still miserable.

He hadn't seen a whisper of Victoria. Not a flash of her glossy green eyes, the rippling of light against her lips, the manner she had of walking as though unaware all eyes in the room were on her.

He sighed as he locked up his cabin door. A sharp northern wind bit into his cheeks and drifted into the cuffs of his sheepskin jacket. Winter was coming. No snow on the ground yet, but the September breeze was picking up and flakes were whipping from above. Strange though. It was mostly a blue sky with scattered clouds. The snow wouldn't last long, he predicted. The flakes were melting as they hit the dirt.

Mother Nature wasn't sure what sort of day she wanted it to be. Hell, he grumbled, it matched his mood.

He turned right at the corner house, onto the boardwalk, and headed for the mercantile to buy wool blankets and other supplies necessary for his new home. Skagway would be his base. After long discussions with John Abraham and the deputy marshal, Brant had carved out a place for himself.

Funny how he thought of this as home. How long would this one last? he wondered. Maybe only till winter passed and the spring thaw allowed the ships to move again across the ocean.

Or maybe longer.

Behind his shoulders, two ships in the harbor blasted their horns, signaling they were close to leaving.

He wondered where they were headed, who on board had found the fortune they'd sought when coming to the Klondike, and who was leaving empty-handed with their dreams shattered. Cooper was likely on one of the ships. Brant had dropped by the clinic yesterday to say his goodbyes and wish the man luck in his schooling in Philadelphia.

Unfortunately—or maybe fortunately, depending on the point of view—Victoria hadn't been there.

But Cooper had, and Brant twitched with pride at the way it had worked out for the up-and-coming doctor. He'd shown stamina and perseverance and had toughened up remarkably. Alaska had done that for him, Brant surmised. It was Victoria's belief in Cooper that had brought out the best in him.

Victoria.

She'd been right, after all, to press Cooper to achieve more. She'd seen something in his medical skills that Brant had been ready to give up on.

Victoria.

Why did the thought of her bring out so much despair in him?

She'd made her choice. Her future didn't include him.

He'd take it square on the chin. But somehow, the emotional toll it had taken on his heart was tenfold harder to bear than any physical fight he'd ever been in.

He strode down the crowded boardwalk, trying not to wonder what she was doing today. Likely saying goodbye to Cooper on the ship, this very minute.

Brant sighed. Good thing he'd said so long to the doctor yesterday, so Brant wouldn't have to witness the blathering and mushiness today.

Besides, he hated goodbyes.

He looked ahead, buried his chin inside the lapel of his sheepskin coat and fought the wind and blast of snow. Then the sun blazed bright and soaked into his cheek. He passed a few folks doing their early Saturday shopping, bustling from the candlemaker's shop into the warm fragrant air of the bakery.

Brant caught the handle of the mercantile door and pushed it open. The bell above his head tingled as he entered. Half a dozen other shoppers were examining the stock on the shelves. A fireplace raged from the corner, enveloping the place in rich, bone-sagging heat.

He headed for the shovels. He'd need one for the coming winter.

"Mornin', Brant," said the man behind the counter.

"Morning, Joe."

A ship's horn blasted from outside, barely audible above the clanging of pots and pans that Mrs. Dewey was creating as she rifled through the shelves.

"It's wonderful what you did, Mr. MacQuaid, in capturing those awful men," she said.

"It wasn't my doing alone. Had a lot of help."

As sleek and flat-footed as a duck, she waddled to the counter with a shiny cooper kettle. "So I hear. Just goes to show you how much a community can do when they work together."

He tested out his shovel. "Um-hmm."

"I hear tell Cooper Sullivan's on that ship," she said as Joe rang up her order on his fancy new till.

"I reckon," Brant replied.

"Along with his new bride."

Brant's shovel hit the floor with a zing. "Pardon?"

"His new bride." She pulled out her coin purse and rummaged through it.

Joe unthreaded the price tag from her kettle. "So the rumor's true. I've been hearing from my customers that it's Miss Windhaven."

Panic hit Brant as surely as if someone had smashed the metal blade of the shovel against his chest.

Not a word from Cooper yesterday. Not a word.

"You must be mistaken."

Mrs. Dewey shook her head. Her white hair, knotted in a huge loose bun, shivered as she moved. "Nope. I got it from one of her neighbors, my sister. He proposed, he surely did. My sister heard it from her window."

Brant flung the shovel back into the corner. It clanged against the others as he pushed past the door and incoming customers.

The ship's horn blasted again and he sprinted along the boardwalk, arms flying at his sides, long legs leaping past pedestrians, horses pulling carts, youngsters playing tag. He sucked in the air but it felt as thick as the ocean, for he couldn't catch his breath and he couldn't comprehend his loss.

Victoria. No!

Which ship was it? He reached the docks and waterside shacks, ducked past people hauling their wares and hollering for him to buy their fish and handmade canoes and imported watches.

Brant grabbed a fisherman by the shoulders. "Which ship to Seattle?"

The man shrugged.

"Which ship to Seattle?" he yelled up at a deck-hand hoisting rope.

"Both, sir."

"Cooper Sullivan! The doctor! Which ship?" he yelled again.

The deckhand wiped the back of his mouth with his gloved hand and pointed to the far one.

Brant raced on board, taking the gangplank two rungs at a time. He gulped down his breath. The tightness in his chest pounded up his throat and threatened to explode.

Victoria stood by the luggage inside the propped cabin door when the whistle blasted again, sending a jolt up her spine.

"You've been on edge lately." Cooper, dressed in a waistcoat and tie, touched her shoulder. "I hope that eases soon."

She pulled her gloved hands together. Her string purse dangled from her wrist, swinging back and forth as the ship swayed beneath her. She'd dressed in her Sunday finest for Cooper today, a damask burgundy suit and skirt. Her tension eased when she looked up into his clear eyes. He'd shaved his mustache, and the clear angles of his jaw gave him an older, sophisticated look.

How silly she'd been to ever think he was too young for her.

She reached up and stroked his cheek. "You're being so thoughtful, Cooper. I'll always—"

Footsteps pounded on the deck outside. Knuckles rapped on the opened door, causing her to turn and frown at the rude interruption.

It was Brant.

He was out of breath. Looking rather beaten, he needed a good shave. Beneath his black cowboy hat, his dark hair was strewn from the wind.

Those deep granite eyes pierced straight through her, reminding her again of the two blissful nights they'd shared together.

The muscles in her legs felt weak. Her arms were heavy and the air on board seemed suddenly thin, too thin to get a good dose of oxygen. Her feelings were too frightening to face, and she was confused as to his presence.

"What is it?" she asked.

"Am I too late?" He swallowed as he watched her expression change to deeper confusion.

And then realization struck her that he must be here to say goodbye to Cooper.

She shook her head. "You're not too late." The heavy curls pinned to the top of her head, topped with a plumed burgundy hat, shook about her ears. "There's still time to say goodbye."

His mouth twisted into something unreadable; he was either out of breath from running, or stunned and displeased that he'd run into her unexpectedly.

His sheepskin jacket parted open. "Are you married yet?"

So he'd heard. A wash of embarrassment flooded her cheeks. Why must he know every personal thing about her? It was bad enough how snoopy the neighbors were, and yesterday, even her patients had been asking direct questions on the state of her personal affairs.

She couldn't tell him. She just couldn't discuss this in front of Cooper. And she suspected Brant's motives. Why did he wish to know? So that he might wish her all the best in her married life to Cooper? It would be too painful to hear those words from his lips.

Or was Brant wondering what might become of the young girl he once knew in St. Louis? Maybe he was pleased another man would take her out of here so he wouldn't have to bear any of their awkward moments again.

This clumsy moment sat like a overripe peach between the three of them; soon it would start to mold. Her eyes flicked to his shoulders, to the door, down at the luggage, anywhere but his face. Then in the tense ensuing silence that seemed to stretch all the way to tomorrow, Cooper finally answered.

Were they married yet? Brant had asked.

"No," Cooper said softly. His gentle eyes looked from Brant to her.

"Good," said Brant, his chest heaving with the breath he'd been holding. He reached out to stabilize himself in the doorway. Was it the sway of the ship that uprooted his balance?

"I need to talk to you, Victoria. Cooper, I hope you don't mind leaving us for a minute."

She stepped forward, the stiffness in her skirt swooshing about her fancy high-button boots. "You can't make Cooper leave. It's his cabin."

She glared at the angles of Brant's face and swore she knew every line there. The grooves around his deep eyes, the way his cheek tugged up when his mouth flickered.

He stared right back at her, as if memorizing the skin he'd traced with his fingers under moonlight and firelight. His intensity stole her breath, like an unexpected thief who took what was most meaningful and left emptiness in its place.

Cooper shuffled behind her, touched her waist

and squeezed past her in the room. "It's all right. I think you better listen to what he has to say."

"Cooper, please stay."

But he just shook his head softly, stepped past Brant at the door. As Cooper passed by, he skewed a look from one to the other, planted a hand at the hip of his waistcoat and shook his head. "You're both just as stubborn as the day we set out on that stagecoach."

Cooper held out his hand to Brant and shook firmly, then disappeared onto the deck.

Victoria stepped up to Brant, her string purse bobbing at her wrist. "Why must you always display your power? Why pick on Cooper?"

"I'm not picking on him," Brant replied. "In fact, I can tell you exactly why he'd make a great husband."

She gasped.

What foolishness was he talking? Was he trying to convince her to marry Cooper? And what business did Brant have of interjecting himself into this moment?

The ship's horn shrilled the air. Seagulls squawked at the noise. A deckhand strolled past the door. "Leaving in fifteen minutes! All visitors to the shore!"

Nervously, she looked down at her gloves and tugged at the fingers.

"Don't do this to me, Brant," she whispered to the whitewashed floor. "Don't embarrass me and try to tell me you know what's best for me, telling me to marry Cooper when...when..."

"When what?" Brant asked loudly and clearly, in sharp contrast to her soft pleadings.

She turned and walked toward the bed. "When you're the last person who should be giving me advice. Especially on marriage."

He didn't respond immediately.

She heard him inhale sharply. When she regained her strength and turned around again, his eyes sought hers.

He murmured, "You won't find a gentler husband than Cooper."

"Please...don't list his qualifications. I know them well."

"He'd always stick by you, that's for sure."

She rubbed her neck and played with the beads on her purse.

"Upstanding young man. Magnificent future. You'd enjoy Philadelphia. Lots to see and do for an intelligent woman like yourself."

"Brant," she urged again. "This isn't fair to Cooper or me. It's none of your business. What Cooper has decided to do without—"

"What's not fair? That I understand why you're intending to go with him?"

She dropped her hands. "With him?"

"What's not fair is that you never intended to say goodbye to me."

Her feet felt bolted to the floor. The ship swayed beneath her and she felt woozy and dizzy. "This is madness. Stop it."

Hadn't he heard? She had said no to Cooper and his proposal.

Must she explain that to him, too? It was her personal business, not his.

Brant readjusted the brim of his Stetson as she struggled to comprehend what he wanted from her.

"Yes, he would make a fine husband," she said defensively, wishing this conversation would end once and for all. What was the sense of dragging it out again? She'd had enough. She was leaving. She leaped over the luggage on the way out the door, her purse whipping about her wrist and her skirts flying.

"Do you want the details? Is that what you want?" She'd lost control of her voice. Anger seared every word. "Cooper promised everything money could buy. The finest house in Philadelphia. He'd take me to the theater and buy me ball gowns by the dozens. He'd send for my folks, he said, if I wanted them to live close by. Is that what you want to hear?"

Brant steeled his jaw as she raced past him. "I

don't blame you for being tempted by Cooper. He's got it all."

The features of his face took on a look of defiance. The angry clench of his jaw, the steely eyes, the force of his posture.

"Almost," said Brant, reaching out and grasping her wrist. "He's missing one thing."

She tried to yank free but his hot fingers locked tighter. She felt the need to get out of here, to bolt past these wide shoulders and the burning memories of their nights of making love. To leave everyone and everything she'd ever known behind her. Brant was so dangerously close to ripping her heart apart that she'd had enough of him.

"And what's that?" Her hat shook when she snapped her head to look up to his bold gray eyes. "What is Cooper missing?"

"You don't love him like you love me."

Chapter Twenty

Brant watched Victoria's mouth quiver with restraint, and he wasn't sure if he was going too far.

"I'm here to tell you the truth, Victoria. The least you can do before leaving is listen to what I have to say."

She swallowed. Her lashes flicked over her cheeks and her burgundy hat framed the flush in her skin and the dewy mist in her green eyes. Even now, in the heat of battle, she looked more appealing and sensual than she ever had.

"You say it's inevitable that I'll desert you. But it's not true," he said. "Only time can prove it. Not words. When you wake up and I'm there every morning by your side for the next hundred years, then you'll know I have no intention of leaving you."

Her eyes shimmered with emotion.

"Yes, I left your sister. But it's a good thing and you know it. How else would I have known what I was missing in you?"

He glanced down at her luggage, the finely matched pieces, and his heart sped so quickly it knocked around his rib cage. He couldn't let her leave without telling her exactly what she'd be missing.

"You're deserting me this time, Victoria. You're walking out on something so fine and extraordinary, it breaks me in two."

She inclined her head; her shoulders softened. He released her wrist and she took a step back.

They both took a breath.

"I'm still a bounty hunter, Victoria. I'm not giving it up. But these dangerous times won't last forever. Alaska's getting new lawmen by the week. The towns are growing. And I had a long talk with John Abraham. He's interested in the same things I am."

She furrowed her brow. "What are you saying?"

"We may work as a team now and again, on the longer trips. We'll keep an eye out for each other. It'll be safer."

"Safer..." Her breathing started to double. "Don't you see? I'm afraid to lose you."

He had to continue, push himself to say everything. "We all have that fear of loss in our hearts. But you know you don't want to ask me to leave my duties behind, Victoria. Any more than I could ask you to do the same."

She pressed her hand against the bosom of her jacket. "I'm a nurse. There's no danger—"

"No?" He had to make her understand. "It was your trip, not mine, that headed us into Glitter Mountain. Like it or not, you needed a bodyguard. You took precautions and you protected yourself. But it was your trip, Victoria, that headed us all into danger."

Somewhat surprised, she took a step back, grabbing the tall poster of the bed.

"If I asked you to leave medicine behind, so that maybe I could sleep better at night, would you do it?"

"No," she whispered. "No…"

A flutter of emotions washed over her face. A soft frown, a tensing of her lips, a slight nod. Was he reaching her? Did she believe what he was saying? Could she see that she faced a storm of danger in her own occupation, yet he would never ask her to give it up?

"Victoria… We went through hell together. All of us, on that journey, and not just from the danger. So much expectation from our families. My father expected me to follow in his footsteps as governor, but I didn't want that. I want a life of my own. Your father wanted you to marry the minister. Maybe Martin turned you away, but deep down I believe you wouldn't have gone through with it, anyway." She nodded gently, agreeing, and he continued talking. "Cooper overcame his father's wishes to become a doctor by discovering for himself that's who he desperately wants to be. Even Dixon was dealing with his father's expectations—in a bad way—and in the end, he succumbed to crime."

Brant clutched her fingers on the post, felt the heat and the uncertainty.

"Don't go," he whispered. "Please. Don't go with Cooper. Stay with me."

She gently lowered her head and stared at their entwined fingers. Even from the side angle, he could see her eyes welling with sentiment.

"Cooper's a good man. But he's not the right man for you. I am. I want you. As my wife. Victoria, I love you."

She said nothing. Her lips were still quivering, her eyes stuck on their woven hands.

He'd never said the words before, and the revelation was empowering. He had to prove it to her.

Didn't she feel it, too?

She had to. Making love to him on the trail the way she did, with such intensity, there had to be more between them than just physical attraction.

She stilled. "I said no to Cooper." It was barely a whisper.

"What?"

He straightened his shoulders. His sheepskin coat seemed to weigh a hundred pounds.

"Cooper's going back to the young lady who lives next door to his family. Susanna Prentiss. He got a letter from her while we were away. Apparently, his absence made her aware of her own feelings for him."

Stunned, Brant tried to soak it in.

"I said no," she repeated, louder. "Days ago. I told him no. Then when he got the letter from Susanna, he realized his feelings for me were misplaced. It was more gratitude, he told me, for helping him with his profession, and admiration for my work."

The lump in his throat grew till he could barely breathe past it. "Why did you say no?"

"Because I told him…I'm in love with someone else."

A sigh escaped him and he knew.

In that instant, the burden from his shoulders lifted. The sorrow that he might never see her again, the grief that had coursed through his body from the moment he'd heard Mrs. Dewey proclaim Victoria was leaving Alaska with another man.

He reached out and grabbed her, pulled her in by both hands, planted those hands on her waist and wrapped himself around her.

He nuzzled her neck, bit the soft flesh, and lightly kissed his way upward, over her ear, her temple, her cheek, until he found his way to her mouth.

They blended together, their lips caressing, his demanding, hers eager to match his own rhythm. Their bodies met at the hips. With his coat parted, she slid into his pocket of warmth and he grew hard instantly, knowing she was close and that she was finally accepting him for all his worth.

Victoria had finally allowed him into her private world, into her soft embrace, the small hollow at the base of her neck, and the breasts that crushed against him, making his pulse beat like thunder.

The ship's horn blasted, startling them both. He laughed softly against the side of her mouth and she moaned in pleasure.

"You're so right, Brant," she whispered. "You're so right about it all. It was my fear of losing you that made me afraid to even try."

He couldn't wait any longer.

"We need to find a minister." With more sensual thoughts on his mind, he pulled her by the wrist and out the door to the deck.

"Tell me again," Brant pleaded, filling Victoria with a heady pleasure.

His words came softly, as light as a feather as she closed her eyes and lost herself in his touch.

"Maybe I won't," she teased him, with a catch to her throat.

"Tell me," he insisted as they lay together on his bed. He kissed the valley between her bare breasts and lowered his mouth, skimming the swell of her tummy and going farther down her body to the secret pleasures he'd shown her in the past twenty-four hours.

"Hmm…"

"Victoria," he threatened in laughter.

"Brant, I love you. I love the way you hold me, the way you kiss me.…"

"That's more like it."

What was he doing now?

Still with her eyes closed, she wondered what part of his naked body was touching her thigh. Was it his mouth? Then it bobbed slightly and she knew it wasn't his mouth. She giggled up at the rafters of his new cabin.

Oh, that.

His erection brushed against her inner leg and dipped against her knee as his expert hands massaged her shoulder, down her arm, her fingers, then along her hip to settle on her thigh.

His touch alone was enough to send shivers of gooseflesh up and down her spine. How could one man have such an effect on her?

This man. The one who cherished her and loved her and held her for hours and hours.

They hadn't come up for air since he'd brought her here, twenty-four hours ago.

His new home, he'd said. He'd bought it for a small portion of the gold he was storing in the bank's vault. This was meant to be his home in Alaska. The one he was now sharing with her.

Before the ship had sailed, they'd said a tender goodbye to Cooper. She'd thanked him for all he'd done for her, and promised to write.

"I know you'll be happy," Cooper had whispered in her ear before sailing out and waving to her and Brant, standing at the shore. "As happy as I'll be with Susanna."

She knew in her heart that Cooper truly was grateful for the summer he'd spent in Alaska.

One she'd never forget, either.

How could she, when she'd met the man she would spend the rest of her days with.

Brant's large hands trailed up the length of her other leg, working from her toes to her calf, the ticklish spot behind her knee, then up to the juncture of her hip and thigh. Such an intimate spot.

She felt his breath at her stomach, quick and warm, then his lips again, tantalizing her with kisses and soft caresses. She marveled at his ability to charm her, his skill in coaxing the woman in her to tell him what she wanted and needed from him in bed.

But this time, no words were spoken. He pressed his body lightly against hers, exploring the chasm between them, while his huge firm hands pressed up along the sheets and gripped her along her sides, kneading her flesh as though she was clay beneath his fingers.

When she felt his warmth near her chest, she reached out with the flat of her palms and pressed them against the acres of manly flesh, the firm muscles of his chest and the taut stirring of his belly.

Trembling, she lifted her knees, parting to allow him to nestle in between them, and couldn't keep her eyes closed any longer. Her lashes flashed open and she took in his slight smile, the messy hair and the soft golden light that reflected from the bedroom fireplace onto his face.

Reaching up, he planted his hands, one on each side of her head, to anchor himself, then slowly eased his shaft along her opening. Hot and ready for him, as she had been for this entire twenty-four-hour session, she moved her hips down and he penetrated her, sliding into the warm sensations and filling her with a sense of love and splendor.

His chest pressed against her nipples, lightly rubbing the soft swells, making her flesh tingle with a bolt of lightning that seemed to connect straight from her breasts to her thighs.

"Umm," he said, reflecting how fulfilled she felt, giving herself up completely to this person she adored.

Her hands came up to his hips, slid along his backside as he pushed deeper inside of her.

He grasped the sheets with his fists for anchor so he could grind himself farther. Her body moved in time with his, their flesh pressed tightly against each other, perspiration mounting as his thrusts got quicker and deeper.

His mouth came down on hers as they moved together, lost in their union and seeking a release to the sexual tension balling up in their muscles.

Faster and faster…higher and higher…getting close to the brim of ecstasy…the pinnacle…and then the final, exalting release.

She came first this time, her whole body engulfed by the thought of Brant, the joy of uniting and expressing her love in the most intimate way imaginable. Her muscles clenched, her body arched in the wonderful ride of bliss that seemed never to end.

"Victoria," he murmured in her ear. "I'm going to make love to you like this forever. Not like you've ever imagined it and longer and fuller than any man ever could."

And then he was lost, too. He pressed his forehead against hers, his chest stiffened, his biceps flexed and he moaned with such abandon it echoed against the rafters and silenced the crackle of the fire.

Toward the end, his rhythm softened. He nibbled the side of her neck and collapsed into a heap beside her.

Smiling in awe at the man she'd conquered, she turned on her side and propped her head on her elbow. He was glorious to watch.

Firelight gave a golden hue to his rough muscles and long legs.

With a sly grin and a glint to his eye, he stroked her cheek. The power of his love graced every touch, every gesture toward her. How could she have ever doubted him? She would much rather spend a year with Brant than twenty years with anyone else.

"Hungry?" he asked.

"Sex and dinner. What more could a person want?"

"Nothing," he said with humor. "Absolutely nothing."

Rolling over, he reached for a towel and tossed it to her, then her robe. When he reached for his own, she voiced a complaint.

"I'd like to admire you for a while longer, if you don't mind."

"How about a few more decades?"

"You've got yourself a deal."

"The water's probably boiling by now. Let's go see."

He grabbed her hand and led her out of the bedroom into the cozy main room. The fireplace was huge, the kind a person could stand right inside of.

A cauldron was heating water. More filled pails, pumped from the outdoors, were sitting by the tub in the middle of the room, ready to be mixed for her bath.

While he prepared the bath, she slipped to a sideboard in the kitchen. Humming, she opened the glass door and lifted one of the china dishes, a speckled blue, from the pile of four.

"Very nice choice, Brant. Feels like home."

She checked the cupboards for food. Cans of beans and sardines and corn were stacked in rows. A bin of apples sat on one side of the pine counter, salt and spices to the other side.

She opened another cabinet and it was stacked with fresh linens and bars of soap. Everything had a masculine feel to it, in its color and design, but she was touched by how thoroughly he'd supplied his new cabin with the essentials.

"You've thought of everything."

He looked up from pouring water. "Only you were missing."

Her throat tightened with emotion. "I'm glad you came after me."

Gently, he set down his bucket and came to stand beside her. She had to crane her neck to look up at his rugged face, and rise on tiptoe to hug him.

He pulled her into his arms, gave her one of his incredible kisses, and then ran his hands into the opening of her robe. She wasn't sure what he was about to do, until he slid it off her shoulders. It fell to the floor at her bare feet. And she was once again bathed in the heat penetrating from the fire. They'd made love in every spot in the house. The bedroom, in front of the fire, the kitchen counter, even up against the front door.

He gazed at her face, then unabashedly lowered his eyes to her breasts. He cupped one in his hands, as though marveling at the vision. A muscle pulled in his jaw.

"You're going to keep me up for hours more," he murmured, much to her secret pleasure. "But first, a bath. Then we'll leave the cabin for just a little while. We need more food," he said, in that gentle tone she adored. "And it's time we tell our friends we eloped."

* * * * *

A sneaky peek at next month...

HISTORICAL

IGNITE YOUR IMAGINATION, STEP INTO THE PAST...

My wish list for next month's titles...

In stores from 3rd February 2012:

- ❏ The Disappearing Duchess – Anne Herries
- ❏ The Surgeon's Lady – Carla Kelly
- ❏ Improper Miss Darling – Gail Whitiker
- ❏ Beauty and the Scarred Hero – Emily May
- ❏ Butterfly Swords – Jeannie Lin
- ❏ Gold Rush Groom – Jenna Kernan

Available at WHSmith, Tesco, Asda, Eason, Amazon and Apple

Just can't wait?

Don't miss Pink Tuesday
One day. 10 hours. 10 deals.

PINK TUESDAY IS COMING!

10 hours...10 unmissable deals!

This Valentine's Day we will be bringing you fantastic offers across a range of our titles—each hour, on the hour!

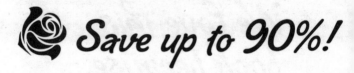

Save up to 90%!

Pink Tuesday starts
9am Tuesday 14th February

Special Offers

Every month we put together collections and longer reads written by your favourite authors.

Here are some of next month's highlights— and don't miss our fabulous discount online!

| On sale 20th January | On sale 20th January | On sale 3rd February | On sale 3rd February |

Have Your Say

You've just finished your book.
So what did you think?

We'd love to hear your thoughts on our 'Have your say' online panel
www.millsandboon.co.uk/haveyoursay

- Easy to use
- Short questionnaire
- Chance to win Mills & Boon® goodies

Visit us Online

Tell us what you thought of this book now at
www.millsandboon.co.uk/haveyoursay

YOUR_SAY